DIM'S ENCHANTED YARD AND FARM TOOL COMPANY

Dim's Enchanted Yard and Farm Tool Company

R.W. KENDALL

To Amy, my mom, and Melissa. Thank you for everything.

Chapter 1

A Self-Stirring Pot Causes Trouble

Dim hauled the heavy iron pot onto the worktable in her shop, wiping sweat from her brow, aiming to get the mechanism right for Mrs. Appleby's order. "Third time's the charm, my little tinkers!" Dim said, with a forced cheer from her mechanical friends.

Her clockwork creatures helped Dim gather tools and parts. About a foot tall each, there were two brass girls and one copper boy. One girl, Glimmer, resembling Dim, mimicking her red hair and whimsical dress, the other girl, named Molly, looked older and wiser and didn't hesitate to show these traits at every opportunity. Little Al, the copper boy, had sculpted brown hair and green glass eyes. Her clockwork children had been her constant companions for years. The copper Tinker watched the pot with disdain, keeping his distance. This temperamental contraption had run amok before.

At first, all seemed well. The pot trembled, then a spoon leapt up, stirring with little energy. Dim grinned, adjusting the speed. The tinkers remained poised for flight, refusing to feel comfort. The copper boy calls out 'just in case' orders in warning to the others.

It was too late when Dim noticed the dial had spun too far, the spoon blurring into invisibility. The pot shook with vigor, tipping over, and spilling the test soup across Dim's floorboards with a crash. The tinkers scattered with mechanical shrieks of terror. They scrambled to get away from the rattling pot.

Dim grasped for her wrench, struggling in vain to re-gain control as the pot tilted onto one edge. Boiling wa-ter, carrots, and chopped celery spilled from its depths, a waterfall of vegetable delight, as it rose into the air!

The pot swooped down and the tinkers dove for cover. Its path colliding with shelves of half-finished gadgets and sending tools flying in all directions. Dim's works-in-progress demolished, gears and springs crushed to scraps. Her creatures hid, watching in dis-may. Glimmer peered out at the wanton destruction.

Dim swept up her stool and swung it at the pot with a cry. Wood collided with metal with a resounding clang, but the possessed pot merely wobbled before righting itself. It swooped in for another pass.

A lucky strike from the whirling spoon caught Dim in the forehead, leaving her stunned. She stumbled back, vision swimming. The possessed pot circled for another pass at breakneck speed. Dim shook off her daze as the pot tilted back at the apex of its climb, poised to come crashing down upon her in a lethal blow!

In desperation, she jammed her shoulder against the massive worktable, straining with all her might to push it aside. The heavy oak table slid into the pot. It teetered in the air after the collision for an endless moment, spoon rattling in anticipation of the kill. With a shout, Dim gave a mighty heave, adrenaline granting her strength.

The table slid as the pot came crashing to the floor where she stood. Its fall silenced the chaos at last, the spoon clattering against metal and wood as the pot lay still. She raised her arms in silent victory, huffing and puffing from the battle. The tinkers mimicked her victory pose. She sagged to her knees amid the ruins of her shop in relief and dismay, anger building even as her heart pounded in her ears.

The tinkers emerged with care, squeaking in dismay at the ravaged shop. Debris and overturned benches littered the floor. The sign 'Dim's Wonders and Gadgetry' - her mother's gift when Dim opened the shop - now hanging askew. Her poor creatures fluttered about the wreckage, unsure what to do in the turmoil.

The gnome clenched her teeth and grabbed a scrap of metal. She brandished it as a club, bringing it down on the remains of the pot with a resounding CRASH.

Again and again, she smashed at the sad remnants of her work. She pounded out her rage and frustration until it was little more than a dented, misshapen lump. Still, it was not enough.

Tears of anger and loss streamed down her face unchecked as she threw aside the makeshift weapon, shoulders shaking with spent emotion. The tinkers gathered around, chirping and whirring worriedly in their strange mechanical language as they sought to comfort Dim with pats of metal hands and snuggles as best they could. Their creator slumped amid the ruins of her livelihood, head in her callused hands.

At the sound of hastening footsteps, Dim looked towards the front door with a scowl, ready to chase off any gawkers coming to stare at the notorious havoc wreaker of the village. But it was Earch who appeared in her doorway, surveying the scene of destruction in shock. He glanced around at the scattered remains of Dim's precious gadgets and half-finished works with dismay writ clear across his face.

Rushing to Dim's side, he gently examined the nasty bruise forming on her forehead where the spoon had struck. "Your contraptions are getting rather...enthusiastic," Earch said in a feeble attempt at a joke that could not hide the concern in his eyes. He helped Dim climb unsteadily to her feet, making certain she was steady before letting her go.

Dim managed a watery chuckle despite herself, anger and frustration melting away under the warmth of her friend's care. Earch had helped patch both her wounded pride and battered shop again after each disaster and setback, knowing chaos and calamity seemed to come naturally in the months since her mother's death. Today's devastation, the worst yet, still left her with a companion who excused the destruction.

The tinkers fluttered up to the newcomer. He was as much a friend to them as Dim, having known him for all of their lives. The copper girl stood shyly to the side, her arms at her hips, her head slightly tilted away. "What happened here, my friends?"

Little Al, who looked like a tiny version of Earch grasped a tiny pot. He Chirped and whirred excitedly, the tinkers mimed the pot flying about the shop and Dim, played by Glimmer, battling the possessed thing in turns. He watched their fervent reenactment of events with no little amusement, interpreting the little creatures' clockwork pantomime for Dim's benefit. Dim couldn't help but laugh at the tinkers' exaggeration of her battle with an inanimate object.

"They seem quite impressed by your heroics and derring-do here today," Earch said, unable to hide the twitch of his lips in a grin as Dim smiled at her creatures' dramatic portrayal, wiping away the last of her tears.

Dim, aided by Earch and the Tinker, quickly repaired the damage and salvaged usable tools, deciding what she could fix or reuse. Anger and frustration had burnt out, leaving her drained and heart sore in their wake, yet her friend's playful teasing and levity lifted Dim's spirits far more easily than pity ever would. After they cleared the worst of the debris, unceremoniously tossing the possessed pot into a junk pile and kicking it once more, Dim felt like herself again.

"When was the last time you slept?" Earch asked as he swept debris off her couch and makeshift bed. He looked her over. "Or ate?"

The gnome shrugged, "Can't sleep." She left the other question unanswered as she sat down next to her friend.

"Or bathed?" He said, holding his nose. The tinkers mimicked his expression and giggled.

"Not helpful."

He looked at her, touching the new bruise on her forehead and removing a stray piece of wood shaving from her hair. She winced slightly. "It may be if you were in my shoes." He laughed, and to his relief, she did as well. "Why don't you clean up and change? We'll get some food and figure this pot out another time."

Dim protested, but saw in Earch's face that he was not asking.

They were going out.

Chapter 2

Zaela's Quest

Dim wrung her hands at the doorway. She was sweating from places she didn't even know that she could sweat from. Earch looked at her and smiled as she wiped her hands desperately on her flowered dress.

"Everything will be fine," he said. Putting his hand on her shoulder.

She smiled up at him. Not a smile she would be proud of. More of an 'eh' smile than one showing any confidence whatsoever. There was a reason that she had not left her house since her mother's death. Her mother had been her confidence. Her reason for adventure. Her reason to take risks. Her rock.

Now that rock was gone. She needed to find that confidence somewhere else, of course. But she was not ready yet.

Then again, she may never be.

She had always known that no matter what happened to her, her mom would be there to make it better.

Dim sighed. Better to get it over with. Earch would not let her out of this. She pulled herself together, adjusted her dress, and wiped her sweaty palms, once again, across said dress. "Okay."

Earch nodded down to her. "Ready?"

"Let's go."

Dim's body, which wasn't particularly raised to begin with, sank and tried to hide away. Her three-foot-five-inch frame tried to shrink into a two-inch hole.

"I knew this was a trap."

"No trap. They wanted to see you."

"I'm not ready for this." She wanted to run, but her legs would not report. "I can't."

Earch touched her shoulder again, pulling her gently to her full height. She felt his confidence build in her.

"These are your friends. There is nothing here to be afraid of, and you can leave in an hour. But," He squatted to look into her eyes, "give them the hour."

"What if I can't?"

"They'll understand." He rose, grabbed her hand, and squeezed it. "You got this," He whispered.

"Like hell," she said, and then giggled.

"I got you."

Dim drew a breath. She painted a false smile on her face and waved to her friends. "This is gonna suck."

"Probably."

"Zaela is going to have some adventure she'll try to rope me into."

"Probably."

"You're very amused by all this, aren't you?"

"Absolutely."

Dim squeezed her friend's hand and looked up at him. She dropped her head to her feet, missing his smile.

Zaela reached her first, embracing the gnome with her slender, elvish arms, enveloping her in a deep hug. "I have missed you, my friend." she kissed her cheek.

Dim let the embrace subside. Zaela was one of her oldest friends, almost as long as Earch. Dim had never seen so much emotion on the woman's face.

She blushed as the hug went on for way too long. "Three seconds," Dim said, even though the gnome had never actually recalled the elf ever touching her before. She had always been so distant in the past. She either truly missed her or wanted something.

Probably both.

"Come here, you little thief."

Dim had a tear in her eye as she looked up. Way up. To the giant, that was Bromm. "You'll never let me live that down, will you?" Dim said, as Bromm lifted her with his incredibly gentle hands. He swung her around with a laugh. Dim could not stop herself from laughing with him. Many feared the giant, because of his size, and truthfully, grotesque appearance. But not Dim.

"Nope, you'll live on as my little thief as long as we both breathe."

He spun her faster, but she felt no fear. Just joy. It was strange, but of everyone, the giant knew her best. They were both outcasts in their own way.

"Put me down. I'm gonna puke." She said. He placed her on her feet. "Well met, my friend. It's been too long."

"Aye," Bromm grunted and went back to his tea. "It has, at that."

Garrick raised his glass to her and smiled as Earch filled a glass for her. Dim raised hers and smiled at the rogue. He winked at her.

Earch refilled her glass every time it became shallow, and she was glad. She would not make it through this without being at least a bit drunk, and the more drunk, the better.

Seeing her companions and telling tall tales about adventures they had had together let her mind rest for the first time in a long time. And calling each other out as they lied and exaggerated when they really could not get away with it made her laugh genuinely. The five of them talked the night away. Dim ate a proper meal for the first time in ages and packed away half for a well-anticipated lunch on the morrow.

It brought her back. Not all the way, but close.

She began to feel the alcohol in her as the hours passed by. Time seemed to stop with her old friends, but she decided she was ready to go. The tinkers would be worried. Or, at the very least, they would have destroyed something.

"I must go." She said to the group.

Groans came from all, but Zaela stood up and embraced her again.

"Hear me out, before you go." She looked into the gnome's eyes. "I'll be quick."

Dim sat, thought for a moment, then twirled her index and middle finger in her tried-and-true way towards the elf. "Let's hear it."

Zaela smiled.

The group sat around the table, finishing their meals and ordering another round. Dim requested a 'to go' box, to the dismay of the rest of her party and the barkeep. But he wrangled a box and slid half of the steak and cheese sandwich into it. Dim's mouth watered as she thought about eating that for lunch. She wanted to devour it now, but she would pay for that later. Best to wait until lunch.

Maybe breakfast.

Either way, she was not paying much attention to her friend, focusing much more on her food.

It had been a long time since she had eaten good food. She had to get out more often.

She looked around and saw that the others were giving their full attention to Zaela, and she felt it may be rude if she didn't at least listen. Even if she had drunk a bit more tonight than she had in the last few months.

She felt horribly tired. Listening was the last thing she wanted to do.

She looked at Bromm and wondered why he always drank that herbal tea. It was gross. Smelled good, but she tasted it once and almost cried.

And Garrick with his whiskey. It was not pleasant.

Earch at least drank good things. She looked at his lips taking a sip. She shook her head and tried to sober up a little, realizing Zaela was still talking.

"So, we haven't been together, all of us, for a while." Dim wondered if she had missed anything and then remembered how much Zaela talked when she wanted them to do something and decided that she probably hadn't. This was the end of the preamble.

Garrick groaned. "Just cut to the chase, elf."

Bromm grunted in agreement as Earch looked on and told them to be patient. Dim just wanted to go to sleep, but giggled. Then she giggled some more because she giggled. She had definitely drank too much.

"I talked to the alchemist down the road." Zaela finally, to Dim's amazement, got to it.

"Jairen?" Dim interrupted, "How is he?"

"Of course it's Jairen. He's the only alchemist around." Garrick said. Dim just shrugged and put her head down. If she didn't leave soon, she was going to wake up here.

"He's good." Zaela continued.

"That's good," Dim said, "He's a good guy."

Zaela glared at the gnome, to no avail. She was almost asleep. She tried to continue.

"How's his Berstidice?" Dim mumbled.

"His what?" Zaela asked.

"Last time I talked to him, he said he had something. I think it was Berstidice or Borstiduce. I don't quite remember. Started with a b anyway," Dim yawned. "Said it kept him and his wife up to all hours."

"Didn't mention it," Zaela said. "But he mentioned a JOB. Did you want to hear about it?"

Dim tried to do the finger twirl, but failed. She tried and failed again. "Sure." she gave up and said, her head still on her arm on the table.

"Anyways," Zaela continued, "the alchemist said that there is a flower that he needs a petal from."

"That sounds easy enough." Said Bromm.

"Should be. Only a day or two, tops. Something to get us rolling again." The elf leaned back and folded her hands behind her head.

"Pay is good?" Garrick asked.

"Very."

"I'm in." the rogue leaned back as well, mimicking the elf.

Earch looked around, "I am not doing much at the moment. I am in, as well."

Dim replied without lifting her head from the table, "I thought that you couldn't, umm, leave due to you being the only mage in the village," she said, surprising them all. They thought she may have fallen asleep.

Earch shushed the others before they said anything. This was not the time to get into it. "I think they'll survive a few days without me."

"Out," Dim said, waving her finger in the air. "I'll be a mess in the morning and the tinkers need me."

The others tried to convince her with no luck. She gathered her things and stumbled from the tavern. Earch tried to walk her home, but she told him to stay. She would be fine.

"I will stop by in the morning before we leave." He told her as she waved to the group. She needed sleep.

A few minutes later, she stumbled back for the leftovers she had forgotten. She could not wait for the wonderful lunch.

Chapter 3

The Fear Gorta

The gnome stumbled into the alleyway behind the tavern and quickly regretted not having Earch accompany her home. She knew that would be an awkward good night and that she may succumb to temptation. That was not how she wanted it to happen. She beamed a bit as she thought about him touching her hair and pulling the straw, or whatever, from it. It must have meant something, but it never seemed to amount to anything either way.

She was too drunk to think of these things now, anyway. It would only result in agony.

As she rounded a corner towards her shop/home, a fog rolled in. It was an ordinary fog, save for its sudden appearance: one moment absent, the next, consuming everything. Dim's heart skipped a beat. Her fingers instinctively reached for the dagger sheathed at her side. She had faced sorcery before, and this seemed to fit the bill.

Rounding another corner and her heart was racing a bit; she cursed herself for going home alone, this time in a complete sense of safety and not, well, passion was as good a word as any. She was confident in her abilities to fend off attack. That wasn't the issue. But she was quite small, a bit drunk, and could be overpowered if surprised. Having someone else to help would not hurt at all. She gripped the handle of her dagger tighter.

Out of the fog, she saw the figure. "Spare a bit of food, lass?" it said. She pulled her dagger in surprise, but the being just stood there. The voice was raspy, as if it had not had a drink in some time.

Dim turned on her heel. Beggars in the village were, well, non-existent. She was sure that they were commonplace in big cities like Grendale and Fisher. But here? The people were not rich by any means and city-folk would definitely think of them as poor. But food was plentiful, and no one needed to beg. At least not for food.

She retraced her steps. The figure was there again. Impossible. Was it another? It couldn't have moved so quickly. "Spare a bit of food, lass?" The question echoed in the fog, its tone and volume unvaried.

The gnome turned again, rounded the same corner, and ran straight into the same figure. "Spare a bit of food, lass?"

Its eyes sank deep into its face. It was skinnier than Dim, seeming to weigh less than her, but it stood at least 6 feet to her at a minuscule three foot five. "You're a Fear Gorta?" She backed off a few paces.

"Spare a bit of food, lass?" it bent toward her now, trying to get face to face. Stretching at a distorted bend, seeming to grow as it slid towards her.

"Of course," Dim said, handing over her leftover food from the tavern. She regretted it a bit. She was looking forward to it being her lunch tomorrow. Fear had set in and although she may regret losing her yummy lunch, it did not matter at the moment. Besides, it looked like the thing wouldn't make it an hour without some food. "Take what you like."

The beggar took the box and rose to its full frame, towering over the gnome. It must have been at least twice her height now, although she'd swear it hadn't been a few moments ago. "Mmm." escaped its lips as it inhaled the sandwich. "Thank you, dear," it said. Its smile was too big for its face. Its semi-toothless grin made Dim think of the pumpkins carved on harvest night.

"May I go?" She stammered, her voice wavering.

"Yer so kind, lass." it bowed to her. She walked past him towards her home. A hand reached to her shoulder. She shivered at the touch, the chill running through her whole body. A vision of people starving in the street passed through her mind quickly and then was gone. The touch froze her skin. She turned to face the beggar. "Your adventure on the morrow will bring much joy to those you love, to all around. But will come with much trial before reward. You must stay true to your ideals. To your friends. There will be pain." It took a bite, its monstrous teeth digging into the meat of the steak and cheese sandwich. It closed its eyes in what seemed pure joy, and continued, "regardless."

She shuddered at the sight. "But I am not going on the journey."

It swept the remaining bits of Dim's lost lunch into its mouth and turned to walk away. "That would be troublesome." and continued in what she would swear to her grave was her mother's voice, "to all."

Chapter 4

The Valley of the Flower

The mage approached his friend's workshop the next morning to check on her before he and the others embarked on Zaela's quest. As he neared the open doorway, two of Dim's tinkers darted about, all agitated, chirping and whirring anxiously.

Dim soon emerged, handing him a large pack. "Could you hold this for a moment?" she said. Before he could inquire further, Dim hurried back inside.

Perplexed, Earch looked to the tinkers for an explanation. Little Al hung his copper head while Molly wrung her brass hands. Suddenly, realization dawned on him. "You're coming with us, aren't you?"

Dim reappeared, now carrying a second, smaller pack. "Only Glimmer's coming," she informed Earch. "the other two know why." The chastened tinkers lowered their heads further.

The wizard laughed. "Causing trouble again?" he asked them. Molly stamped her foot indignantly but offered no defense.

Dim called out "Bor! Come 'round front, boy!" An over-sized tinker came clanking into view, laden with supplies. Dim began strapping on her packs. The ox-like tinker puffed steam from its neck, where a head would be if it had one.

Earch raised an eyebrow. "Are you certain that you want to bring him? It will only be a day or two. Three max, Zaela said."

"Why? Don't you like him?"

The mage shuffled, "It is not that I dislike him. He is fine. But something always happens with him."

"He's got a new leg spring! I replaced it last night." Dim said proudly. Bor lowed in agreement.

"Did you sleep?"

"I told you I can't." Dim disappeared and grabbed a few more bags, loading up the ox. "Aren't you supposed to be back at school, by the way?"

"Do not change the subject to me."

"Aren't you?"

He had tried to put this off, he still wanted to. "I will go back next term."

"This better not have anything to do with me. I can handle myself." As she said this, she fell over, trying to strap a bag on the ox.

Earch laughed. "At least bring the others. Little Al and I get along so good." The tinker dropped to his knees and put his hands together, begging Dim to take him.

"They have a mess to clean."

"In your house." Earch's eyebrow raised again. Dim could not help but laugh.

"Fine."

"Molly can stay." The mage teased. Molly was having none of it and smacked him in the shin as she jumped on Bor.

With Dim's massive packs and Earch's simple bag, they began walking down the winding village streets, Bor plodding heavily behind. Glimmer perched on Dim's shoulder, chirping excitedly.

Soon they reached the edge of the forest where Zaela, Bromm and Garrick awaited. Zaela hugged Dim fiercely and helped secure her packs. Dim wondered why the elf had become so affectionate.

"What did you bring in all this?" Zaela asked, eyeing the bulging bags.

"Bits and bobs in case I need to fix anything." Dim grinned. "And snacks."

Zaela laughed. "Naturally, I don't know how you stay so small with all your snacks!." She turned to Bor. "Ready for an adventure, old friend?"

The tinker ox lowed again and tapped one hoof impatiently.

As the group headed into the trees, Earch walking beside Dim, he asked, "Do I want to know what's in your 'bits and bobs'?"

Dim grinned mischievously. "Probably not." She said. "But I promise no explosions this time!"

Bromm roared with laughter from up ahead. "That is usually the best part of our quests!"

Dim called out, "You say that now!" as Garrick chimed in, recalling how they had nearly burnt a duke's home to the ground, with Bromm reluctantly using his tea to extinguish the last flames.

"That was excellent tea." Bromm remembered, "Expensive. I think you still owe me for that."

Dim prodded Earch's side. "See? Maybe we can burn down a prince's house this time!" The prospect of danger, strife and calamity ahead could not dim her spirit. Or her friends' irrepressible joy in it all. With a chuckle and a shake of his head, the mage looked to the forest path ahead, wondering what misadventures this journey would bring. Hopefully, not too many. This was supposed to be quick.

"Onward then. Then." Earch said with a sigh and a smile.

The travel was steady, uneventful, and truthfully quite boring. The valley was not all that easy to walk to, but it was close to the village and other settled areas. Besides a few large morothes and an occasional hempin or two, there wasn't much for the party to worry about. And Bromm scared most of those off on sight, anyway.

The small valley was carpeted with wildflowers of every hue but one - the rare silver moon rose, blooming under the light of the full moon, stood out from the rest. The flower seemed to glow from within as it filled the valley with its sweet perfume.

Guarding the beautiful rose were hundreds of iridescent Rig-lo bees, obediently hovering around its delicate petals.

"Remember, we must only retrieve just one petal," Zaela reminded the others. "Any more could kill the flower."

Dim wasted no time pulling gadgets from her seemingly bottomless packs. "This smoke machine should distract the bees long enough for us to grab a petal." She quickly cranked the handle, filling the valley with thick purple smoke. The high-pitched constant buzzing that the bees made lowered in pitch and slowed to a hum.

"Now Garrick!" Zaela said. The rogue crouched low and began sneaking quietly toward the silver moon rose. But as he neared the perimeter of the bees, he sneezed. This was not a normal sneeze that a person would typically make. This was the most high pitched, incredible sneeze you would ever hear. Another followed it. And then another.

Bromm could not hold it in and started laughing. "That's the wimpiest sneeze I've ever heard."

Every bee in the valley instantly turned as one, ignoring the smoke and swarming toward the source of the disturbance. Garrick sprang up and began swatting at the bees descending upon him.

The rogue turned and ran, sprinting as fast as he could toward the tree line. Angry bees gave chase. The high pitch returned. They followed him deep into the woods where they began relentlessly trying to sting any exposed flesh.

The companions watched helplessly as their friend disappeared from view, being chased by the bees seeking vengeance for disturbing their sacred bloom.

Before the others could react, the giant Bromm strode purposefully into the midst of what remained of the swarm. He smashed several out of the way as he made a direct path to the silver moon rose.

"Bromm, stop!" Zaela shouted. But the barbarian ignored her plea, pushing on through the smoke.

The elf turned desperately to Earch. "He's going to destroy the flower!"

Earch tried to reassure her. "Bromm knows we only need one petal. He'll be careful-" But his own words betrayed his uncertainty.

As the purple smoke subsided, Bromm emerged, fighting off the angry bees that swarmed around him. He spotted the others and held up a large silver petal, smiling triumphantly.

Zaela, Earch, Dim and the tinkers saw a massive swarm of bees gathering into a buzzing cloud behind Bromm, hundreds, maybe thousands, strong and seething with rage. They descended upon Bromm's oblivious form.

Bromm felt the first bee land upon his skin, and he was instantly in a full sprint. He flew past his companions before they could react, besides Glimmer, who dove and grabbed onto Bromm's leg, floating into the wind like a flag. She saluted the others as they began to move.

"Little stinker. She can't even get stung!" Dim said as she grabbed Bor's yoke, Molly and Little Al as Zaela pushed her on top. This was not the first time they had to flee in a hurry! Zaela and Earch were running full speed once the gnome was on her way.

The furious bees gave chase, following the group deep into the forest. Their angry buzzing filled the air as they pursued their quarry relentlessly.

The companions fled through the dense undergrowth, dodging trees and leaping over roots. Their breathing grew heavy, but they dared not stop. The buzzing had dulled a bit, but was still there.

Soon they came upon a steep, grassy slope leading down to a lake below. As Earch, Zaela and the Dim hanging onto Bor slowed at the edge, they could hear Bromm groaning as he slid to the bottom. After a moment's hesitation, Earch shrugged towards Zaela and they were running, then quickly sliding, and just as quickly tumbling down the slope after Bromm. "Hells!" Dim kicked at Bor, who gave a gruff snort, then followed.

The slope gained speed. Rocks and tree roots whipping past in a blur. Bor was in a full belly-slide as they hit the water with a massive splash, coming up soaked with Dim breathless. The bees had stopped following at the top of the slope, staying to guard their sacred bloom.

The group checked on each other, laughing, and splashing water with relief upon seeing everyone was okay. Bruised and battered, but Okay. Bromm produced the sizable silver petal, eliciting cheers.

Bromm tucked the silver petal safely away and splashed at Zaela, who was not expecting it and took a substantial amount in the nose. She gasped a bit and looked down her nose at the brute. "I'm sorry! I didn't..." Zaela then tackled him under the water. Glimmer began a quick back stroke as Molly raised her hands in frustration. Bor found safety on the land with Little Al.

Garrick emerged from the trees, covered in welts and stings. "So glad you were all so concerned for me," he said sarcastically. The others obliged him with some splashes.

The sun rose, painting the sky deep red and then fading into blue. Although the day was just beginning, they were in no shape to travel after the bee ordeal. They stayed the day to mend their various cuts and stings.

The group made camp. While Dim and Zaela (along with the tinkers, minus Bor, who seemed to take a nap in the grass) started a fire, Garrick and Earch went fishing. Bromm seemed to disappear for a bit, then came back with a large dead tree and preceded to chop it with his maul.

Molly retrieved Dim's blanket and pack and set Glimmer and Little Al down for a well-deserved nap. Then she climbed in next to them.

"Do they even sleep?" The elf asked Dim.

The tinkerer ate another snack. "No, not really. But they like to pretend." She wondered what was going on with the elf. She was being very clingy. "Bor seems to nap a lot, but I don't think he needs to."

"They take after their creator."

"Not lately. I haven't slept well in weeks... months, maybe."

"You need a distraction. That's why I invited you." Zaela leaned back and ran her hand through her hair. "And I missed you."

"Missed me? I never thought of us that way." Dim turned away.

"No, you're right. But, I don't have many," she turned away for a moment, "any female friends. You're the only one I can stand."

"Is that why you're being, well, a bit more touchy feely?"

"Sorry." She blushed. "I was told that I am too stand-offish. I'm trying to work on it. I can stop."

"I don't mind, but be yourself. At least with me. I like you the way you are."

Zaela smiled.

Eventually the fire was going strong with Bromm's wood. The tinkers were at least in a pretend sleep and the boys were scaling the fish they caught.

When the fish was done, the five sat around, eating and drinking. Bromm delighted in a tea Dim had brought along, finally forgiving her for the waste during the fire she had started years before, and began twiddling a shape from a block of wood he had gathered.

It was much like the old times, as they shared a day at the lake. Besides the bees, they did not have the dangers they were used to, but the companionship was there again. As the night came, Zaela shared her blanket with Dim (the tinkers were stubbornly refusing to give up Dim's own.) The sun went down in a mimic of the sunrise hours before.

Four of the five, eight of nine, if you count the clockwork tinkers who were pretending, drifted off to sleep. The one holdout was Dim.

This was her biggest fear of coming along. Well, this and the typical dangers that came with adventuring. Staying awake and finding something to do alone in her house caused no problems for anyone else. Getting up and doing her own thing while everyone was sleeping was a different story. She was not lying when she said that she could not sleep.

There was the occasional twenty minute or hour long doze off here and there when she just could not keep her eyes open or her body shut down. But that was about it. Sleep that was once filled with beautiful, impossible dreams was now filled with darkness or horrible nightmares. The darkness scared her more.

Tonight was neither.

She laid next to Zaela for a for a few hours. The elf put her arm around her while she slept. It was foreign to Dim. Her parents were very loving towards her, but never the hugging type. Touching anyone gave her an awkward feeling. She tried to roll herself out of the blanket with as much stealth as she could. She failed.

"Where are you going?" the elf asked sleepily.

"To pee. Go back to sleep." Dim tucked her friend back in. Something was up with Zaela, but Dim could not put her finger on it. Now was not the time to find out, as she heard the elf start a melodious snore. Dim paused. She could listen to that sleep song for hours, but she needed to be busy.

Grabbing one of her packs of bits and bobs, she moved a ways away from the group to try not to disturb them. She found a small clearing overlooking the lake where she could see the waters turn to more of a bog in the distance. She took out what appeared to be a regular lantern and cranked the handle. It did nothing until she swore at it and slapped the bottom.

Then it lit up.

Looking out over the waters, she bit into a formed bar of oats and granola that her mother had taught her to make and watched as the wills danced across the way.

"I know that you're there. You might as well come out."

Glimmer showed herself and sat next to the gnome. She pointed towards the wills.

"Just some gasses over the boggy areas. People think they're faeries and wander to catch them sometimes." She took another bite of her snack and pulled out her tools. "Usually with terrible results, mom used to say."

Dim worked on projects through the night until Molly and Little Al shyly came into the clearing.

"What is it, my friends?"

They gestured and mimed and, on more than one occasion, needed to be shushed in fear of waking the others.

What they were trying to say was that Bor was gone.

Chapter 5

Some Strange
New Gnome and
a Wooden Box

The four of them went to where the mechanical ox had been napping since the morning before. It was easy to track him. He was not sneaky.

That was the good part.

He was very heavy and plowed straight to wherever he planned to go without hesitation.

That was the bad part.

Although Dim, and now Glimmer, knew of the dangers of the wills, Bor did not. That was the direction the ox had taken, towards the glowing, dancing lights. And the bog.

The ragtag group, led by a frantic Dim, only because she was about two and a half feet taller than the others and moved faster, ran through the woods, following Bor's destructive path. She could not believe that she had not heard this in the night. He could not have been silent. He had only turned when he could not bully down what was in front of him.

They made their way into an increasing tangle of trees as the lake became shallow. The brush pulled in as the environment changed.

Prickers struck her exposed skin and blood shed down her arm.

Her boots began to stick into the mud as the morning light gleamed into the woods. A clearing came, as did what she feared.

First it was the distressed sounds of the mechanical ox lowing.

Then the sight.

Or, more importantly, what she could not see.

Bor sank as he struggled, buried deep into the bog from what she could tell.

Tears welled in her eyes.

"Hold still, Bor! We're coming."

But her yelling had the opposite effect than what she wanted as the ox tried to turn towards her voice, struggling and rearing.

He sank more.

"Molly, Al, get the others." Dim shouted, "Glimmer with me!"

Little Al immediately began running in the wrong direction, only to be corralled by Molly. They ran full speed, which was not quick, back towards the crew. Glimmer smacked her head, both at Little Al's mistake and the fact that she knew what was coming next. She has not happy about it.

The gnome scurried through her bag. She pulled a fifty-foot rope and made a loop on one end.

Glimmer shuddered at what Dim removed from the bag next. A crossbow.

It was a small, 'hip shooter' her father had once called it, a crossbow that he had made her to bring her hunting when she was small. At least smaller than she was now.

She ran her hands over the oiled oak wood of the weapon, surprised that it was still in such good shape. Her father was a great woodworker, having many of his creations still adorning the village shops a decade after his death. And a decade and a half after, he could still work as well as he once did.

But he had made this one special. Just for her.

Glimmer backed away as Dim loaded the crossbow with a special bolt she had made years ago. The tinker knew what was coming, and she wanted no part of it.

"It's not that bad," Dim said, without looking up from loading the bolt. She fastened the hooped rope to it, as well as another smaller rope.

Glimmer pointed at Dim, almost poking her.

"I can't, you know that. You wouldn't be able to pull me back."

The brass girl pointed to where Molly and Little Al had gone and shrugged her shoulders.

"We can't wait for them. Al could get lost and Bor has little time." She finished securing the bolt and tied the smaller rope around Glimmer. "I know that you're scared, but it's the only thing I can think of. If Bor goes under, we may never find him."

Looking side to side, Glimmer gave up. She could not think of a better idea. Her shoulders dropped and she let out a fake, exaggerated sigh.

"I'll get you back. Hold tight."

The tinker did and closed her eyes. The gnome raised the crossbow, aimed at the sinking ox, and fired.

A brass streak flew through the bog towards Bor, missing slightly to the left. The tinker splashed into the muck. She gave a glare to the gnome, who laughed and shrugged her shoulders.

Glimmer swam to the ox, wrapping the loop around the beast and secured it.

After petting her friend on the back, reassuring him, Glimmer pulled on the smaller rope.

Glimmer sank as well. Something was wrong.

She pulled again.

Nothing.

She sank more and struggled to climb onto Bor.

She pulled again.

Again, nothing.

She looked towards where she had launched from. Glimmer tried to focus and cleared the muck from her eyes. She looked again. Dim was there but fading from view. The crossbow dropped from her hand and the tinker watched her try to pick it up, to no avail. Someone else phased into view and then they both disappeared where they had stood.

"What the Hells?" Dim yelled, as the crossbow melted from her hand. The surrounding lands changed from the woods in the sunrise to what she could only be able to describe later as a burnt wasteland.

The lake and bog were still there, but of a strange color. Glimmer and Bor were no longer in sight, although she thought she saw an outline of them for a moment as she concentrated. The trees were different. And dead. Everything here seemed dead.

She was in the same place, but not in the same place at the same time. Dim looked around her, but everything was a daze. It was as if she had just awoken from a deep sleep and her eyes could not focus.

At first only the dead trees, the lake and bog were around her. As she looked around, the visage of another gnome took shape. This would not be too scary or interesting most times, except for the fact that she had never seen another gnome in her life. He was old, maybe older than old. Ancient came into her foggy mind. She stared at the gnome for too long. Her mind took time to react.

"You're... a gnome."

He laughed, "Yes. And you are Dim, of course."

"I've never seen another gnome before." She stared at him in amazement.

"Odd. I have seen many Dims before. All a little different. Mostly the same, though."

Dim tilted her head at the new gnome. He was putting his pack on. She shrugged and grabbed what had come with her to wherever here was. "How many Dims..." she started.

"I've not the time to explain now," he said as he pulled Dim to him.

As he did, a giant claw crashed into the mud, just feet away from where she had just been. It was so gigantic that she thought the claw, which was at least three times her size, was the danger. Of course, it was a danger, but what it was attached to was a much, much bigger danger.

The monstrous creature, at least three stories high, pulled itself up through the bog. Its scaled shone it what light was around them in a black, silver and red tint that mesmerized her. It flexed its mighty bat-shaped wings that seemed endless. Its mouth showed countless teeth, all to a point, each as large as Bromm. She wished her friends were here now, then she didn't. No need in them all being eaten.

The roar that escaped its mouth deafened and stunned her. She could move no part of her body. Her thoughts went from those of her friends to only running away. There was nothing else in her head except fear and running. But her legs would not move.

Its gigantic head moved towards her, and fear and running turned to despair. She was, at that point, in her

mind, dead. When the despair passed over her, however, she felt a strange sense of calm. If she died here,
right now, she was okay with that at this moment.

Dim wished that she was not stunned so much that
she could not even attempt to defend herself. Maybe
lift an arm or something. It would not do any good,
she knew, but at least it would be something. Instead,
she was just standing there, waiting to be eaten. Probably soiling herself. She could not really feel anything,
so she could be. She would not blame herself. It was
incredibly scary to be almost eaten by some gigantic
thing.

She closed her eyes, thinking 'great eyelids work,
but arms and legs don't,' and waited. Dim thought of
all those tales of the hero who faced down the savage
beast and single-handedly defeated them. She loved
those stories as a child, but now called B.S. Like the
grand knight Bilwog who saved the princess from the
Sacrificer of Cadancer the Old with one dart. Pft to
that, she would say now.

She noticed that she may have been thinking of this
for way too long and that she was either now dead or
something may have made her not yet dead. She gave
a command to open her eyes, which failed at first, but
after another few tries, worked them apart.

She was not dead yet.

The ancient gnome had pulled her into some cavern
of sorts. The smell was absolutely wretched and Dim

almost wished she had been eaten, but she figured she might as well see where this all would get to.

"Can you move yet?" an impatient and grumpy sounding (maybe that was not fair, she did just meet him and he had seemed to have saved her life just now. But did he not bring her here in the first place? She was not exactly sure.) voice said.

"What the Hells was that?" Was all Dim could say.

"Dragon."

"Dragon!"

"Dragon."

"Dragon?"

The ancient gnome nodded.

"Dragon." She said, defeated. Of course, she had heard of dragons. There are tons of myths of them as protectors, terrors, killing virgin girls (why is it that a monster would really care if the girl was a virgin? She had always thought. Also, why was it always girls? Sacrifice some boys once in a while), and as hoarders of shiny treasures. They did remind her of cats, except without the wings and all the people killing. Mouse killing though. Some of the older villagers told tales of their great grandparents seeing them occasionally as well.

A roar and a tremor came from overhead, most likely dragon related. "We should go deeper into the caves."

Dim thought of many questions to ask, like: Where they were? How they got there? Who are you? Why should I follow some random guy? And the like, but all she could say was "okay," grabbed her pack and followed. She figured there might be time for questions later on.

They traveled fast through a meandering labyrinth, crisscrossed with streams beneath the bog, and dragon above. She lost track of her passage many times and tried to figure out how to go back, since her leader was very old and wasn't keeping his breath very well.

Finally, they made it to a larger cavern that the gnome must have used as a home. The rumbles and roars from above had subsided, and her new companion crumpled into a chair. Dim flopped to the dirt floor upon her pack. Although it contained many metal and odd-shaped pieces, she always arranged them in blankets and a pillow so she could drop herself down if needed.

After her host caught his breath, he offered her a cup of Gaettywine. This was another thing she had heard of in legend, but never seen or tasted for real. She accepted, took a sip, and instantly regretted it. Then she took another. It somehow was repulsive and irresistible at the same time.

"Most Dim's have questions around now, do you?"

Her eyes narrowed at him. "Well first, you've said that you've met other Dims before. What does that mean?"

He mimicked her look. "Exactly what I said."

"Are they all like me?"

"No, no. Some are smarter, more confident, more successful, taller..." Dim's glare burnt into him, "or... the other way. I am sorry I don't talk to many people these days, and they all seem to be Dims. I have to meet another soon, so we do have to get this done."

"Why?"

"What do you mean?"

"Why are you meeting so many... Dims?"

"Oh, that, to destroy my hut, of course," he said, as if this was the most obvious answer in the world. "Have you been?"

"Been where?"

"To my hut?"

She was utterly confused by now. "I don't think so."

"Great!" he said and rose to his feet.

"Okay, let's forget the hut right now." Dim pinched her nose.

"Don't forget the hut. That's important."

"Just for a minute. Where are we?"

He looked at her as if she were clueless. "Between worlds. I thought the dragon explained that."

"No. No, it did not." She drew a breath, "I did not know that there was a 'between worlds.'"

"Great!" He said.

"How is that great?"

"It's great for me. I've been looking for the right Dim for... well, I don't really know for how long." He fumbled through his bag.

Dim was about done with this and wanted to just leave, but since she did not know where to go, she had to stay. "So, there are multiple worlds?"

"Infinitely many, I think. I don't know, but I haven't run out yet."

"Am I some sort of chosen one?" She thought that if he had gone through all this trouble to find the one true Dim, maybe it was a prophecy or something, "To save the world or something?" The older gnome just laughed. This was simultaneously comforting and up-setting to her.

"What about my friends? They were sinking in the bog."

The ancient gnome looked at her, puzzled for a moment, "Oh, the brass thing and the beast. They'll be fine."

"How do you know?"

"I am a wizard, for one." He pulled some unimpres-sive box from his bag, he looked at it with a bit of dis-taste. After turning it a bit, he shrugged his shoulders, "and time does not move all that well here for another. It gets kind of stuck. You should get back about the same time you left." He turned his nose up at the box in his hands, "here take this," and tossed it to her.

"What is it?" she asked, taking it from his hand.

"A wooden box."

"I can see that."

"Then why'd you ask?"

"I just..."

"I do have to say that it is usually much more impressive when I give it to a Dim. A majestic sword, a
ring of great power, some sort of glove. Usually not a
wooden box. We'll see, never judge a man by his beard,
my father used to say."

The world around her started to fade away.

"I must be going now, many more Dims to give gifts
to."

"What do I do with it?"

"With what?"

"The box." Dim pinched her nose.

"You'll figure it out."

"Who are you?" The bog was coming back into view,
and the gnome was shifting away.

"Gallila, I think, in your world. Though I have gone
by many names. Oh, and if you do get to my hut..."

She didn't hear the end. She was back at the bog.
Her crossbow was at her feet and she looked out to
where Glimmer had been. She was there, but now on
top of Bor. The whirring was barely audible from where
Dim stood, but she knew they were angry whirs none-
the-less. Glimmer was not happy.

The tinkerer looked around her, fearful that the
dragon would be there. Waiting for her to return. Was it
a dream? She thought that it could have been, except
for the wooden box she held in her hand. After a moment of waiting for the dragon to eat her and listening
to Glimmer's squeals, she decided it did not matter at

the moment if it was a dream, another world or some-thing else. Her friends still needed help.

Dim picked up the crossbow and wound it. It jammed. Glimmer's hands raised and then slapped her sides. Bor seemed unperturbed. He may have been asleep. But he is a tinker, so probably not. Either way, Dim thought that she heard him snoring.

The gnome smacked the crossbow and tried to wind it again. The rope pulled Glimmer into the bog, but it jammed again, making both of them angrier.

Dim paused and took a deep breath as Glimmer struggled and sank deeper into the muck. "Give me strength and save my friend," the gnome said. She took another deep breath and let it out slowly. Dim barely felt a vibration in her pocket where she had placed the box. She cranked the pulley again, and the lever spun with ease and a force she had not felt in the bow be-fore. It surprised her and the weapon fell to the ground, still cranking.

"Hells," she said, as she dashed to retrieve the cross-bow. It flipped and flopped in the mud as the lever spun faster and faster. Glimmer took to her feet in the bog, hanging onto the rope for dear life, riding the wa-ter as she moved faster and faster.

Dim finally secured the bow in her hand, almost be-ing swept into the bog herself. She steadied herself just in time for Glimmer to slam into her midsection.

The next thing that she knew, Earch was looking down at her, flicking water in her face. "What's the trouble?"

Glimmer was trying to explain what had happened to Molly and Little Al, with little success. Molly seemed suspicious of the truth of the tale, while Little Al seemed to not really care. He was chasing a dragon-fly around the bank.

"Right now, Bor."

"I got him." Said Bromm as he picked up the rope that Glimmer had tied around the ox. "It will be slow, but I'll get him out."

"How did he even get out that far?" Zaela asked.

As Bromm pulled the ox from the guck with the un-welcome help of Garrick while Glimmer tried to explain Dim's disappearance to Molly, Dim explained what had happened to all non tinkers as best she could.

The description of the dragon mesmerized them, al-though Dim felt she did it no justice. This was the only spot that Bromm had seemed interested. "Wish I was there for that!" was all he said between grunts.

She talked about the wizard, and Earch seemed piqued. "What was his name?" He asked.

"Gallil, or Galileo. Something like that."

"Gallila?" He asked. His look almost scared her. It was a look that conveyed that it intrigued him, but also that he thought she was crazy.

"Do you know it? I've never heard it before."

"Maybe. I'll do some research when we return to the village."

"Okay." She did not mention the wooden box, or that the crank seemed to take a life of its own. She wanted to test that out before she revealing it.

"This hut? Did he mention much about it?" Zaela asked.

"Not much, something about a Dim getting rid of it." She tried to think more, but most of the conversation was now leaving her mind. Much like a dream after you wake up. "He was vague."

"As most wizards are," Earch finished.

Chapter 6

The Automated Snow Flinging Shovel Thingy

She turned the box over in her hand, still not knowing why she hadn't told the others when she first received it. A little over a month later, she felt it was too late to tell them now. 'Besides, it hadn't really done anything,' she lied to herself. Still, she had not let it leave her side since.

She had an inkling that it had to have something to do with the fear gorta that she had seen, although she had not seen it since. Maybe she never did. Extreme lack of sleep could do that to a person. She may have imagined the whole thing. That would mean, however, that she had thrown away a perfectly good sandwich, and she was having none of that thought.

Also, it would mean that she's losing touch with reality. Not as bad as the sandwich thing, but still something she was not ready to accept.

Earch knocked on her door. She knew it was him because he really was the only one to come to her door anymore. There were no customers (not that there were many before) since she had shut down making new gadgets while experimenting, with little success, on the box. He learned to knock first after just walking in once and receiving a black eye from a runaway spring. Lucky he kept the eye, really.

"Come in, chicken."

The door opened, and a snow covered mage entered. He shivered. "I am just trying to keep all of my original body parts as long as possible." Dim quickly dropped the box into the pocket of her dress. "Are you ever going to tell me what that is?"

"What... what is?" Dim said, scrunching her face. "It's snowing already?" She changed the subject.

Earch just shook his head, but let it be. "Looks bad, too. A month and a half early."

"I hope the crops get in."

"It is not looking good. Many will freeze tonight if this does not change. It seemed to be summer a week ago."

"It was summer a week ago." She threw a log on the fire, suddenly colder.

Earch shrugged. "I have finally heard back about your friend."

The gnome tilted her head to one side until she realized what he was talking about. She was so fascinated with the box; she had almost forgotten about the man who had given it to her. Truth be told, he was slowly fading from her memory, anyway. Probably intentionally.

"Gallila." Earch said. Dim nodded. "Turns out he was a Gnomish Tinker-Mage from about eight centuries ago or so."

Dim sat down and dropped her head into her hands. "So my mind is going, eh?"

Earch sat next to her and put his arm around her shoulder. "Not necessarily."

"Gnomes live longer than humans, but not that long."

Earch patted her back. "True, but he was a tinkerer, and a mage. Marrying those two arts may give him the ability to extend his life."

"Over eight-hundred years?"

"You said that he told you that 'time worked differently' where he had brought you."

"Are you just humoring me now?"

"No," He said, but not convincingly. It did not help. "Look, I believe you."

"Could've fooled me."

"I believe you," he repeated, putting his hands on her cheeks and looking into her eyes. "I do." He began to say something else, probably something that would totally convince her that he did not, indeed, believe her. Something that started with 'but' and continued to say something about not getting enough sleep and 'minds playing tricks on you when stressed.' Things that would not have gone over well with Dim at all. But the tinkers saved him.

Little Al came through the room with a sled while Molly tried to stop him. Glimmer was trying to get anyone's attention as she looked out the window, hooting and hollering on.

The mage and tinkerer went to the windows and saw what they were going on about. The snow had to be at least a foot and a half tall. Everything was white. The snow flew sideways as the wind blustered on.

"This has to be magical." Dim said.

"I sense no magic except what is in your pocket."

The gnome gave a look that the human knew well. He had not crossed the line yet, but he was close. He did think about poking the bear just one more time, but he did not want to walk home in whatever this was.

She began closing her storm windows while taking the sled from Little Al. "Not tonight, maybe tomorrow," she said as the boy stamped his foot and ran from the room. Molly looked smug.

Earch went to get his cloak slowly. Biding time in the hopes that Dim would offer shelter from the storm. She did not disappoint. They had a gruesome meal of some sort of stew and hard bread. They talked and drank throughout the night as the storm grew worse and slowly subsided. Neither spoke of Gallila, what happened, or the box.

As usual, Dim slept little. They had talked and drank until they had passed out in her bed. She woke after about an hour and laid on a roughly four-inch piece of her mattress. Earch had procured the rest for himself. She stayed in bed long after she knew she was not going back to sleep; her mind was on the crops. Without them, it was going to be a tough winter for the village to get through.

Is this what the fear gorta had warned her about? If so, going on the adventure did not seem to help in any way.

Earch's arm flopped across her face, stinging her. She pushed it off. "My damn bed." She said under her breath. Glimmer stretched and yawned in her miniature recreation of Dim's bed, pretending that the gnome woke her. Dim gave her a sideways glance. She was still a bit tipsy and was having none of the tinker's shenanigans without some coffee. Stoking the fire, she put a pot on.

The brew worked its magic and Dim was at least ready to try being productive. She found her winter clothes buried deep in a closet and threw on her coat and mittens. Grabbing her shovel, she then forced the front door open through the snow. It almost came up to her shoulders. She let out a deep breath and shoveled the snow from her porch.

She did not get very far.

After about an hour, she had barely made it to the steps. Everything hurt. Inside, she had another cup and pulled out her sketch pad. A design she had thought of a few years ago came to mind, although her original idea was for the digging ground. She drew it out. It had a pulley and three shovel heads. The pulley was connected to gears to change the power settings, providing more torque or speed if needed. You could even switch it to not turn and use it as a regular shovel.

She proudly wrote 'Automated Snow Flinger' on the top. Looked at it again, said "Garrick be damned," and added 'Shovel Thingy' at the end. She laughed at herself and went to build the device.

Glimmer and the rest were excited to see her working and offered their help wherever they could. Molly directing traffic as she liked to do. Dim decided on two major changes to her initial drawing as she built the contraption. Fourteen different torques and speeds were just too many. It would be too heavy and she just did not have enough gears to do it. Also, it seemed like overkill. Three (one for heavy, one for medium and one for light snow) seemed like enough.

She also put one of her winding gadgets on to make it automated. She hesitated to do this because of all the failures that she had had lately, but decided it was worth the risk. At the rate she had shoveled, it would be spring before she saw the street again.

Dim got the device to the door and out. The tinkers gathered around as usual when she was trying a gadget for the first time, with Little Al taking the necessary precautions behind Molly. Earch moved slightly and gave a bit of a snore of approval. The gnome wondered how he could have possibly slept through all the racket.

Winding the gear that powered the shovel to max, Dim reached into her pocket and gripped the box without thinking. "Please, let this work." She said out loud. It was more for her confidence than the snow. Her friends would help get her free if she needed. Bromm could probably remove it all in a few minutes. But this was the first real inspiration she had had since her mother had gotten ill. The first thing she had really made for herself and not commissioned from a customer since then. If it did not work, she may have to find something else to do. Maybe adventuring full time. Adventurers rarely succeeded very long here, however. They usually had to move away to find any real fortune. Or they went mad. Or died. Adventuring was not a simple game. Although, neither was inventing.

Dim realized that she was stalling and sighed. It was time. She flicked the switch to low and felt the Automated Snow Flinger Shovel Thingy start up. It began to turn. It began to shovel. It began to move the snow!

It threw the snow directly into her face.

She turn it to off and went inside, stomping and mumbling to herself. "Stupid gnome, that was obvious."

The tinkers moved away from her quickly. They knew that she was in no mood to be trifled with.

Dim banged around, finding a sheet of metal and an old stovepipe. It was not in the best condition, but would do for now. She could fashion something better later. She pulled her mallet and got to work bending the metal. Earch rumbled, but did not wake at the noise. She envied his dedication to slumber.

She attached the plate and pipe to the Automated Snow Flinger Shovel Thingy and adjusted it to target the snow to the side and turned it on again. Success on the lowest speed.

Dim pressed her luck, touched the box again, still unaware that she did so, and turned the speed to medium. The device shook a bit and rattled. The whirring noise bumped up to moderately loud. And it still worked!

She was about halfway to the street in no time and decided that she should try to push the invention. The tinkers went inside through their tiny door, cut into the main one and shut it. They took their places in the safety of the windows.

Dim subconsciously touched the box again and felt it vibrate. She closed her eyes and turned the switch. It pulled her forward with a lurch and she panicked, reaching for the switch, but missed. She put two hands back on the Automated Snow Flinger Shovel Thingy and held on with all her might, envisioning disaster.

She got control and held her ground. It was not out of control. The whirring brought some of her neighbors to the door for a look. This time Dim did not feel that they were looking at her to see disaster as they had many times in the past. She did not notice them at all. Tears froze to her cheeks as she cleared a path to the street and kept going.

Earch finally woke with a stinging headache and a strange whirring sound that seemed to fade away and then storm back at odd intervals. After a bit, he realized he was not at home and helped himself to some coffee. Not his favorite, but he needed something. Too perhaps, but he knew that Dim would have none, except for what Bromm would drink. He would not think to drink Bromm's tea.

Looking around, he saw no sign of his friend and figured that she went to her actual bedroom or for a walk. It hit him then. As far as he knew, Dim had not been in any other part of the house in many months, and she certainly was not going for a walk in the snow that fell. It would be almost as tall as her. He looked around and saw Glimmer staring out the window. He looked to the passage to the rest of the house and saw that she went in there, but not to sleep. A few things had been pushed aside, but seemingly only to get through and back. As he looked back to Glimmer, she waved him over. She seemed to smile.

He grabbed his coffee and went to where Glimmer was. At first he saw nothing but snow. The sun glared off of it and blinded him until his eyes adjusted. It looked as if a path in the road was appearing, but it could have just been his eyes.

Then he saw her. Or at least her head. The snow was too high to see the rest.

She was definitely smiling.

No laughing.

The mage had not seen her truly laugh since the lake during their adventure. Before that, he was not sure.

It looked like she was skipping. Snow was flying all around her, but from the ground. She went through the street from one house to another, clearing their paths. Waving to people she had not talked to in quite some time. They all looked at her with a look that said she had finally lost the plot, but they waved back. It was late afternoon when she finally stopped and came in.

"Having fun?" The mage asked.

"Absolutely."

"You must be freezing."

Dim thought about it. She wasn't cold at all. Sweaty, but not cold. "No, I guess all the work kept me warm." She put her new gadget by the door.

"What is this thing?"

"The Automated Snow Flinger Shovel Thingy!"

"Garrick will hate that."

Dim nodded, a little too much. She could not stop smiling.

He looked it over. It was rough, but she had made it this morning. It certainly did the job by the look of the street. "Everyone will want this."

"I can make more tomorrow. I need to get out to the farms and see if we can help."

"I will get the others. We probably can not do much, but we will try."

"I'll get this wound and meet you at the tavern."

Before he could leave, Dim jumped up and hugged him.

"That is not like you," Earch said, squeezed her and placed her on her feet. He went to grab his cloak.

"Maybe Zaela is rubbing off on me," Dim said as she went to the snow flinger.

Earch gave her a look as if he had no idea what she meant. He shrugged and left to get the others.

Dim could not believe that she did not have to stop to wind the device all day. She opened it up and was absolutely shocked to find that it did not need to be wound at all. It was as tight as it could be.

She reached into her pocket and touched the box. It felt warm.

Chapter 7

Dim's Enchanted Yard and Farm Tool Company

"We're going to have to work on the name." Garrick said after they had done all they could at the farms that night. Dim's invention certainly did not save the fall crops, but it let more people in to help. There was much more work to do and it would be a lean winter, but not as bad as it could have been.

"I like it," Zaela said, touching Dim lightly on the shoulder, then almost falling over. They had all been drinking heavily since the owner had said everyone could drink for free that night. He was now regretting it.

He thought that the giant might drink the bar dry, even though he had only ever seen him drink tea. But it was the elf and the gnome. They were like two bottomless pits.

"Another toast." Earch said. He wished he could have indulged some more, but the night before and the work of the day had wrecked him.

"Yes! Another round, too!" Dim yelled and promptly succeeded in falling over. Zaela tried to help her up. And fell as well.

"Oh no. No more!" The owner yelled.

"I'm celebrating!" Dim said back.

"Celebrate at home. You're drunk."

Dim and Zaela simultaneously stuck their tongues out at the owner, who just waved them off. They laughed hard and hung on to each other.

"We should build more things and start a company." Zaela said, as if this was the greatest idea of all time. She pointed at Dim, missed, reconfigured, and pointed again with an eye closed. "You build the thingies, Garrick can sell the thingies, me and Bromm can deliver and show the thingies," Garrick gave her a look, "Earch can... er... do some magicky thingies." She hiccuped. "It'll be great."

"I don't even know what's powering it?" Dim said.

"Yes, you do." Earch replied.

She looked at him confused, then went wide-eyed, "The box?"

"If that is what is in your pocket, then yes."

"Maybe the box." She stared off, something was lost in her.

Earch went to her. "The design makes it work. The box is a magical power source."

"You knew that?"

"It radiates magic." There was a very long silence.

"Can I name the company?" Garrick said, breaking the silence. "Or at least not have the word 'thingy' in it?"

"Garrick gets to approve the names!" Dim said, ending her brief melancholy and throwing her hands in the air.

"You won't remember that." Garrick said.

"Sure I..." Dim stopped, thought for a moment, "No, I won't." She laughed, then jumped up, "Bromm will though!"

They all looked at Bromm. Bromm looked up and raised his thumb.

"And you're good at naming things!" She finished.

"I'll see tomorrow if this box thing..." she stopped herself, "device, can power other thi... stuff too." She winked at Garrick. "You think of a name."

"And I'll get this one home." Zaela turned with an arm around Dim.

"I am not sure you are the best escort." Earch said.

"What's gonna happen? No one will be out in this snow."

The two women left, sticking their tongues out at the owner as they reached the door. He waved his towel at them and laughed. At least they stopped drinking all his booze.

A mist had taken over the village as they walked, holding onto each other for support. They rounded a corner and shivered as the wind hit them. In the distance, a figure appeared. Zaela paused and readied herself.

"Relax, I think I know him." Dim told her and patted the elf's shoulder.

"Really? you sure?"

"No, but I think so. If he asks for food, it's him." She said and waved with enthusiasm. "Hey!"

When they reached him, he said, "Spare a bit of food, lassies?"

"Told you! This is him!" She told Zaela. "How have you been?"

"Spare a bit of food, lassies?" Was his reply.

"Okay, okay." Grabbing the cuff of the creature's long coat. "Come with us. I have something at the house."

"Are you sure about this, Dim?"

She waved her off. "Yeah, yeah. He's fine. We'll give him some food and he'll tell us stuff." She began walking, but the fear gorta did not move. She tugged twice on the cuff. "Come, come. I at least have some bread."

He followed them, Zaela keeping a watchful eye on the long, slender man. The fear gorta was dark, almost a shadow, with exaggerated limbs and neck. He wore a long coat and a wide-brimmed hat. His mouth, when she could see it, looked too big for his head. He was incredibly skinny.

They got to Dim's house, "Come in! I have something, I'm sure." But the man would not move. "Fine, give me a moment, then."

Zaela went with Dim, "What is that?"

"Fear gorta." She said, as if it was obvious. She rummaged through her pantry.

"What the Hells is a Fear Gorta?"

Dim found an old loaf and a bit of cheese, looked at it, picked some green off, and nodded. It would do. "Um... a spirit thingy. They tend to come when there may be a famine or something." She debated giving some of her ham, but she loved ham. She stared at it for a bit, then decided that, no, she would keep the ham. Maybe have it later. "They like food."

"Obviously." She ran her hand through her hair, "So, there is going to be a famine."

Dim shrugged at her. "Maybe we'll find out." She moved towards the door. "For you, sir." she bowed and offered the food to him. She nearly fell over.

"Mmm..." He said and took the cheese and bread. "Thank you, dear," and bowed back.

Zaela saw the teeth in the creature's mouth and shuddered. They were like knives.

"Any news?"

It took a bite of the bread and smiled a wide, fearsome grin. "You have helped." He took another bite and continued, "all."

"Great!" Dim said and did a mini jig. The creature took another bite and turned, fading into the fog.

"We need more wine." Dim said as she looked at Zaela's concerned face, watching where the fear gorta had been. She went into the forsaken parts of her house in search of some spirit. The tinkers looked at Zaela in awe. They had seen her before, of course, but never in this state. Being a wood elf, she never dressed in what city-folk would call the finest clothes, but for the village, she usually had everything together. Tonight, she seemed, well, a bit off. The tinkers did not know what to do with that, so they did nothing and went deeper into the house.

Dim returned with a bottle of something that was definitely old and had no label, and raised it to Zaela. The elf turned to her and forced a smile before a genuine one appeared on her lips. The visitor had taken her aback, but he was gone now. And she was still here.

Pouring the drinks, Dim looked up to the elf. "I like us together. We should do this more often."

"I agree," said the elf, and she leaned in for a kiss. Their lips met awkwardly, and she feared the gnome would pull away, but she didn't. She braved pressing stronger and slipped her tongue into Dim's mouth. Dim giggled.

Zaela pulled away. "Was that okay?" She asked.

"It tingled."

"But," she could not think of another word. "Okay?"

"Yes." Dim was turning a deep red and fumbled for her drink. "I have never been kissed before." She turned her head away.

"Never? I would have thought that you and Earch..."

"No. You're the first."

"Can I be the second?"

Dim looked up at her and nodded. Zaela leaned in and pressed her lips to the gnome's, embracing her shoulder and pulling her (she hoped gently) close as the front door opened to Garrick proclaiming, "We have it."

The women pulled away from each other quickly and grabbed their cups. "We were just having a drink. Do you want some?" Dim stuttered.

"A drink, huh?" The rogue said and then moved away for Earch to make his way in. Bromm ducked through and stood awkwardly, bending to fit.

The two gave themselves more space between them. Dim was redder than she ever was and kept stealing glances at the elf.

The silence seemed to go on forever as the five of them looked at each other. Well, four. Bromm was just trying to get comfortable.

Finally, Zaela plopped herself onto Dim's makeshift bed and patted the side. Dim flopped next to her, giggled, and took a sip. "So what do you have?" Dim asked.

Garrick looked at the two, then at Earch, then at the two women again. He shrugged and poured himself a drink, offering some to Earch, who could not seem to take his eyes off the women. "The name."

"The name of what?" They said in unison.

"The company."

The women looked at each other and then burst out laughing. "Oh, yeah. I forgot."

"It was an hour ago." Earch stated. He crossed his arms in front of him and turned away.

"A lot has happened since then." Zaela said. "Some beggar came by and stuff."

"And stuff." Dim said, smiling.

Garrick cut Earch off before he said anything. "Yes, yes. I'm quite sure that we will hear about the 'stuff' later on. But I came up with the name!"

"Name of what?" Dim and Zaela said together. They giggled again, which did not seem to bode well for Earch's demeanor.

"The company."

"What company?" The women burst out laughing, tears rolling from their eyes.

Garrick tapped his foot and folded his arms. Coming here tonight, obviously, was a mistake. "I'll just tell you tomorrow," and he turned to go. Bromm blocked his way, as he felt it was time as well.

The women got up and went to Garrick, pulling him. "No, tell us. Please." They said, both looking up with what he would call 'puppy-dog eyes.'

The rogue almost gave in as Earch left in a huff, but the women broke into laughter again. He sighed, "To-morrow." He went through the door. "You are going to love it," as he closed the door behind him.

Chapter 8

Bromm and a Very Long Talk

She could not determine if the pounding was on the door or in her head. All she really knew was that it woke her up. Either way, she was not happy about it. Dim sat up and instantly regretted that course of action, flopping back onto the bed. The pounding returned. It was the door.

"Go away." She whispered. Praying that the sound may make it to whatever horrible being was on the other side of the door. It did not. The pounding returned.

She looked around. Molly was staring at the gnome in a nightgown with a very stern look on her face. Dim laughed, then winced. "Can you get the door?"

Molly sighed in quite an exaggerated way that showed her displeasure. She went to the door, jumped to the handle, making Dim laugh again, and pulled down. The door swung open.

Garrick walked in, shaking off the new snow. The breeze coming from outside felt great on her skin. She tried to remember everything that had happened last night, but everything came in bits and pieces.

Garrick looked irked. He never really ever got to a point of looking mad, but you could always tell when he was irked. Dim buried herself in the covers. She vowed to let no one in again.

"You're alive."

She grunted.

"Everyone's at the farms. Get up."

She grunted again.

"Your 'Thrower of Snow' helped, but there is a lot of work to still do."

She peeked an eye out of her blanket. "What?"

He grinned, "The Thrower of Snow. I renamed it."

Dim sat up, rubbed her temples. "Flinger of Snow?"

"No."

"Why not?"

"Won't sell as well."

"Really?"

"Yes." He said, walking to get Dim a glass of water. "You said that I could name things." She squinted at him. "I can get Bromm to remind you."

"I remember... vaguely." She took the water and gulped it down. Handing the glass back and twirled her fingers, motioning for more. "Well, I remember everything vaguely."

Garrick handed her some more water. "That's why we came by last night, to tell you we came up with a name for the company." Dim's eyes went wide, more came back to her. "If we are still doing that?" Her head tilted to the side in confusion.

"There may be some bridges to repair." Garrick continued, "Anyway, Earch and I... and Bromm too, I guess, came up with 'Dim's Enchanted Yard and Farm Tool Company.' What do you think?"

Dim downed the second glass of water and handed him the glass again. "I love it."

"Good, Bromm already started designing a sign. You would have had to have been the one to tell him."

She looked around, seeing Molly and Glimmer trying to clean while Little Al found ways to do nothing. "Where's Zaela? She didn't walk home last night, did she?"

"Hon, she's already in the fields. Been there for hours. Said that you passed out a bit after we left, so she tucked your drunk arse in and finished the bottle. Played with Al and Glimmer until the sun came up and went to work." He looked over at the boss tinker. "Might be what's bugging that one." Molly was not happy about being called 'that one.'

"I can't believe she's working. I can hardly move."

"Elves have incredible stamina." He walked the glass to the sink, attempted to find a spot to put it, gave up and put it on the counter. "So, the Thrower of Snow should sell well. You should make as many as possible to make some quick cash."

"I need Earch to help me figure it out."

"Then you're going to have to work on that. He did not seem happy last night."

"Why?"

He looked at her and saw her tilted head again. He shook his own head. "You're really not good at relationships at all, are you?" Her head position did not change. She scrunched her face. It looked to Garrick like it hurt. "Romantic relationships?"

Her head straightened. "Never had one."

"Really?"

"Yes. Never really thought about it."

"Really?"

The gnome gave him a look. Not her confused, tilted look, another look that if he had given it, she would have said that he was irked. He laughed and saw the look get irkier. "I'm sorry. I thought you and Earch had at least dated at some point. You've always been so... close."

"I've known him all my life." She stared into the distance. "I always kind of thought of him as family. Like a cousin."

"I don't think he was on the same page, hon. You may have to talk with him." He sat himself down in front of her. "Before we go, winter is a good chance to build a reputation. Our biggest problem will be the Spring. That is when Mallory will notice."

"Madame Mallory?" Dim's eyes went wide.

"She won't be happy about competition."

"No. No, she won't."

"Get dressed, hon. There's work to do."

There was lots of work and Dim suffered through it all. She kept her distance from Earch. Zaela as well. And Garrick. She kept seeing him looking towards her and grinning. She did not know if he was laughing at her, but it certainly seemed so. Knowing that it was not malicious did not make the gnome feel better.

Dim stuck with Bromm for the day. She liked Bromm. He talked little and listened well. He gave expert advice that was simple and easy to understand. They both agreed that simple was best, which was not exactly what the other three thought.

Bromm is a giant of a, well, I would say man, but he is not exactly human. He does not even know, or at least has never said, what he is. He stands over nine feet tall and probably weighs upwards of 750 pounds. His features are absolutely hideous. A visage that would, could, and has created nightmares in grown men.

The people of the village would call him a 'gentle giant.' None of them have seen him smashing bullins or goblins with his maul as Dim has, though. They would probably not be calling him 'gentle' if they saw that.

He did not drink alcohol, which was odd for an adventuring sort. Also odd for the village. It did nothing for him, though, so tea was his drink of choice. It was much cheaper, although harder to find. He had discovered tea on the same day that he met Dim and was drinking his first cup when he saw her and Zaela try to pick the pocket of a witch. He had watched in amusement until the gnome was in extreme danger. They had been good friends ever since.

Bromm loved children, because, although they were scared of him at first sight, if he gave them one of his wood whittling creatures, they would normally accept him for who he was. He loved Dim because of this, too. She had no objective like the others, she just accepted him.

That was Bromm, a good guy all around. Unless you crossed him to a point that he could not accept. Then he smashed you with his maul.

I have not talked of Dim's conversation with Earch, mainly because it was boring and consisted mainly of 'umm's' and 'you know's' along with many confused looks from Dim and other what-nots.

If you have ever had to have a conversation where one of you had a long-standing crush on the other and now was quite upset that they had gotten drunk and kissed your friend, or had a conversation with someone you thought was just your best friend and had absolutely no idea that they had some sort of feelings for you and you could not understand why they were mad at you because you have never had those feelings for anyone ever, well you don't need an explanation.

If neither of those things have ever happened to you, then you can probably just think of Dim's reaction of being as a child who was being continuously asked why they did something by their parents, without the parents telling them what it was they did, and they had absolutely no idea what their parents were talking about.

In the end, as happens a lot in these cases, nothing was really resolved. Things never got back to how it was between any of them, but they never really do. People change and adapt. We'll see how all that plays out as the story unfolds. One part of the conversation you should hear, though, is this:

Dim asked, "Why have you not gone back to school? I'm fine and can handle myself."

"It is nothing to do with you."

"Then why?"

Earch sighed and straightened his cloak. "I blew up the library." He whispered. The others were within earshot, definitely eavesdropping, but trying to look like they weren't.

"What?" Dim asked, although she had definitely heard.

"I blew up the library. Are you all happy now?"

Dim and the others laughed. Earch turned red. "How?"

"Fireball." He mumbled.

"Fireball!" Garrick said. "In the library!"

Knowing he could not get out of this now, Earch just got on with it. "One of my classmates dared me. They said the library was fireproof."

"Was it?" Dim asked.

"No."

With that, Bromm spit out his tea and laughed harder than anyone had ever heard him before. In fact, his laughs were usually a grunt. But that day he laughed. It brought great joy to everyone, even Earch, to hear it. Although, for the mage, he did not realize the joy until it was but a memory.

Chapter 9

Winter Well, A Sign, and Some Visitors

The winter was harsh. Food was scarce, but sufficient to feed the village. The people did not eat well, but they ate. The snow was unrelenting.

Business, however, was tremendous.

Dim and Earch worked together to figure out the wooden box. It ended up being quite simple. Cast a small enchantment and the gnome's gear would self wind. Put an on/off switch or trigger on and there-ya-go, self powered tools. After that it was just a matter of build a tool, cast a spell and deliver to the customer. Garrick seemed quite bored, since the Throwers of Snow needed no salesman. He helped where he could, and devised a plan for the spring, but he really needed something to do.

Dim was too busy building to notice. Nor did she notice the tensions that were building in their little group. Nor did she notice Zaela's flirts or Earch's advances. She may not have noticed even if she was not so busy building, but the business made her even more indifferent to this new aspect of her life.

For the most part, when she finished a tool, Earch would enchant it. Dim would leave him to his work and if Bromm was around, she'd brew him a tea. She'd grab a glass of wine and sit with her friend as he whittled away on another gift for the children of the village. They loved his animal sculptures, and waited around for the new edition, whatever it may be.

They would sit in silence on the back porch after a quick 'thank you for the tea' from Bromm. This time, though, he was not there. She could have sworn that the giant had been there, and she did not want his tea to get cold, so she called out to him.

Little Al popped his head around the corner of the house. "Have you seen Bromm?" He looked back to the front of the house, still with his hands on the corner, looked back at Dim and shook his head feverishly.

"What's going on?" Dim started walking towards him.

He came to her now, waving his hands in front of him and hooting and whistling. He got directly in front of her and grabbed her hand, trying to lead her to the back. "Bromm's tea is getting cold. You know he hates that."

The giant's voice bellowed from the front, "It's fine. Be there in a minute."

"Now I know something's up!" Dim yelled, but allowed it when Little Al took her hand and walked her back to the porch, where she sipped her drink. They sat in silence and waited. It was almost the same as sitting with Bromm, but not quite. She relished the smell and cool breeze of the almost but not quite spring air and let them do whatever it was they were doing.

"I'll have to get started on the 'dirt digger upperrer thingy' and the 'grass cutterer and remover' soon. Then we'll need some reaping machines. Not much more snow coming, I think.." she said mindlessly.

Little Al whirred a bit in agreement, looking over the horizon as if predicting the lack of coming snow. Then he scratched his chin and nodded. "What are they doing up there?" She asked as she heard Glimmer grunt in dismay as something fell and made quite a loud banging noise.

The tinker just shrugged his shoulders, but seemed to giggle. Something was up.

The gnome grew restless as they sat for a few more minutes. "What in the Hells are you doing up there?" A bit more angrily than she intended. Patience, sometimes, was her strong point, but not when she felt she was the only one not in on a joke.

"A few more minutes." yelled Zaela. Dim pouted.

"A hint?" she asked Little Al.

He made some sort of expression that he really only made when Molly had threatened him. She never really followed through with her threats, except of course that one time she did, and Little Al never forgot that one. Dim sighed, then went in for another glass. 'We really need no more Throwers of Snow,' she thought as she poured extra.

A few minutes later, she was called to the front. She wanted to walk with purpose, showing that she was not excited to see what the big secret was, but she was almost at a sprint by the time she turned the corner.

A large sign now hung over her doorway. A beautiful, gigantic wooden sign with large fire-burnt letters.

"Dim's Enchanted Yard and Farm Tool Company" it said. Glimmer hit a switch, and it lit up somehow. All of her friends smiled at her. All she could do was grin a stupid grin and turn beet-red.

"It looks won-der-ful." They all heard, and all turned around to find the person who the voice belonged to.

The voice's owner was a bit more than a foot taller than Dim, stood leaning on her cane, admiring their sign. A woman, if met anywhere with no knowledge of her, would be a beacon for some offering to help her cross the street. A woman who with no prior warning would strike fear into no one.

A woman known as Madame Mallory.

Two, well I guess henchmen would be the best word, flanked the cronish looking woman. One was about as wide as Bromm, though much shorter. He was only about seven feet high. The other was a slender woman. She could have been mistaken for an elf with a quick glance, but further inspection saw that she was not. She was playing with a dagger as a child who wanted to poke a dead squirrel with a stick, but knew her mother was watching and would not approve, would play with it.

"I hear you had a wonderful winter." The woman said. The voice was that of an old woman, but held authority. It commanded attention.

The friends froze. Glimmer nearly fell from the sign. Dim tried to speak. Felt nothing come out, cleared her throat. Still nothing. Cleared her throat again and replied in what she had hoped was a powerful voice (it was not) "It was okay." And then shrugged stupidly.

Mallory moved towards Dim. She was obviously used to towering over someone in terms of authority, but seemed uncomfortable towering over someone in stature. She struggled to look down at Dim.

"I heard it was outstanding."

Dim swallowed hard. She never met someone who clearly commanded such... well, she did not know. She never met a woman like this. "I'm not sure. Better than my gadget shop ever did."

"I'm sure." Mallory said. "Let me in for a talk?"

"My workshop is a mess," Dim said. "Not fit for company."

Mallory looked into the gnome's eyes. "It's fine, my dear. I am sure that I have seen worse."

Dim shrugged.

"Let's have a cup of tea," Mallory added after a pause.

Dim looked to Bromm, who nodded. The slender hench-woman looked Zaela up and down, then did the same to Earch. The brute moved to the door. Bromm blocked him.

"No need." The woman waved the brute off. "It's just some tea and a talk."

The two women went inside as the others looked each other over. Dim went straight for the kettle. Mallory waved her off as she did her brute. "I have no genuine interest in your tea, dear."

"No."

"Not at all." She said, looking around at the dilapidated work area. "You look like you could use some money."

Dim saw where this was going and put the kettle on, anyway. She stood in front of it as it boiled. "I don't."

"But dear, this house is…"

"My house is fine. Could use a bit of cleaning…"

"A bit…"

"Yes, a bit," she said, stronger than she intended. She knew this was an important conversation. Not so much what was said, but how what was said was said. "I can build something to do that." She paused, as Mallory spoke, she interrupted, "easily."

Mallory seemed a wee bit taken aback but recovered quickly. "I am sure that you can, but I am not interested in your inventions and..." she picked a small gear up, glanced at it with disregard and then tossed it aside, "gadgets. I am interested in the power. I will pay dearly."

The kettle screamed. Dim motioned that she could not hear the woman, but did not move to take the kettle off the stove.

Mallory nodded and smiled. It was not the loving smile of a grandmother that she resembled; it was that of a wolf. She turned to the door. "I will see myself out."

"Make sure that you do." Dim said, not sure what that meant, just happy that the woman was leaving.

Chapter 10

The Reaperator 3000

"Any luck?" Dim asked Garrick as he pushed through the door, ringing the bell that hung over it. She beamed for news, but her eyes showed that she knew the answer already.

Garrick hung his coat on the hook and looked around. "The tinkers have been doing great, keeping this place clean."

"They have been a bit more active since business picked up."

"As are you, hon."

Dim raised her newest invention, the Tree Cutterrer Downer, although Garrick would inevitably change the name (even though she left thingy out) but then realized he was avoiding the question. "How did it go?"

Garrick sighed deeply. He really wanted to keep hope up, but it was getting tough to keep slinging hope when none came back. He was running out of hope ammunition. It was quite worse when he spotted the tinkers peeking around the corners. Their moods and Dim's seemed to mimic each other. He couldn't explain it if he tried, but the force of the four emotions was quite formidable. He spied the cat-thing that had appeared late in winter. "What the hells is that thing anyway?" he asked.

"Don't ignore me, rogue. I know your tricks." She went over to the mangy creature and gave it a pat. "No clue though, but Little Al took a liking to it and it stayed."

Little Al took that as a cue to walk over to his friend and pat him as well. Dim had come home one night late, and the thing was there. The creature was quite like a cat, but with eight legs and it did not, at least that she had heard meow. It purred regularly though and ate well. It even let Little Al ride it occasionally.

"You don't have to hide it. Just tell me what's going on."

Garrick sighed. "Well, sold a few small things. Met with a few of the big farmers."

"And..."

"And nothing. They won't switch, hon. They are 'happy' with what they got." He used finger quotes. Dim giggled at him. It was new to her to see him so frustrated.

"But our stuff is better."

"That's not the argument."

"Then why are they so 'happy' with what they got?" She mimicked his finger quotes and let out another giggle. Glimmer did it at the same time and got a scolding look from Molly.

"Something to do with Mallory, probably."

"I thought she was out of town."

"She is, but her muscle isn't. My opinion: they are threatening the farmers to stay with her equipment. That, or after the slim winter, the cost to change is too high." He took his boots off and sat. Dim brought him an ale, and he thanked her. Little Al made a waving motion by his nose. "You can't smell. Leave me be." He looked up at Dim, questioning if the tinker could indeed smell. She waved him off.

"But we're selling the small tools?"

"Yes, hon, we are. And it is keeping us afloat. But without at least a farmer or two coming on board, we won't really 'make-it.'" Finger quotes again. Another giggle. Garrick gave her a look and saw Little Al doing the quotes to the others. He kicked towards him and he scuttled away. The cat thing stood up and gave the rogue a glare. Garrick sipped his ale. "We'll just teeter between closing and making a small profit."

"Much like the gadget shop." Dim flopped into a seat. The tinkers, in their own way, followed suit. The energy was gone.

Garrick nodded. "I think our best bet is Appleby. She seems like the only one who might defy Mallory. They have been at odds for decades."

"I've done a lot of business with her. She was friends with my parents. Maybe I should speak with her?"

"Couldn't hurt. She sees right through me."

"I bet. She's a tough cookie." Dim settled into her chair. The not quite a cat snuggled onto her lap to get her fair share of petting. "I'll go in the morning."

"Did you want company?"

Dim thought a moment, then shook her head. "No, I think you'll scare her off a bit. I need to call in a favor for this one."

Bor was not happy to get up. He had been in pretty much 'nap mode' since the ordeal at the bog, but Dim needed him to carry the sample tools. She would have asked Bromm to carry it, but Mrs. Appleby was a mistrusting soul who did not take kindly to strangers. And although she had seen Bromm from time to time, Dim was pretty sure the farmer would not be as welcoming with the giant around. Everyone else she would think of as 'sketchy adventurers' at best.

No, if she wanted to get the business moving, she had to do this one alone. Well, kind of.

After loading the sample Automatic Soil Tillerator and the Reaperator 3000 (she had asked Garrick what the 3000 was for, but was only told that, in sales, a high, round number was great, so she went with it) into her dad's old wagon and got Bor oiled and wound, she saw the three tinkers sitting in their old seats. She had not used this wagon in a while, but they used to take it out often, and the tinkers were thrilled.

Molly sat stoutly in the middle, Little Al being held by her (so he wouldn't fall out) to the left, and Glimmer, not sure if this was a good idea or not, teetering between sitting and getting down. "It's fine Glim, Mrs. Appleby is sure to remember you three." She thought for a second about one incident at the farm, shook her head and said, "I'm sure she won't remember the last time."

They rode the long road to the Appleby farmhouse. It was one of the more remote farms in the village, and by far, the largest. It had been in the Appleby family for as long as they kept records in town. There were some rumblings that the current Mrs. Appleby would sell soon, as she was the only known family member left.

Most of those rumors said that she would sell to Mallory. Mainly because she was the only one around who could afford it. Then she would have a near monopoly on the tools and the largest farm. Most people did not think of that, but Dim did. It could change the village forever.

At the end, there wasn't much she could do about that, but it didn't mean that she didn't think about it from time to time. And a semi-long cart ride definitely was a time for thinking.

She watched as Glimmer pretended to steer Bor (who didn't actually need steering. He was fine) and Little Al kept trying to take the reins from her. She'd slap his hands away as Molly sat between them, trying to keep a prim and proper appearance. It was like she was bringing her rambunctious children to church and was trying, with all her might, not to smack them both. In the end she did smack them and Dim had to get involved to break up what almost became an all-out brawl.

"You three need to be on your best behavior. We need this to keep the company going." She paused and looked at the tinkers she built so long ago. "I need this." Dim tried to sit like Molly, but inside she was jumpy and sick to her stomach.

Bor turned onto the path that led to the old farmhouse that had stood all the 22 years of Dim's life, like it was going to fall to the ground. It hadn't yet though, and probably would outlive her if Mrs. Appleby did not sell.

As they got to the house, they saw Mallory's henchmen, the large brute and the slender woman, leaving and a clearly upset Mrs. Appleby yelling at them from the doorway. She was larger than when Dim had last seen her and much purple-er. Probably because of all the yelling. She did not look healthy.

"We'll be back." The slender one said calmly as the brute yelled things I would not say here. It was bad. I would say he swore like a sailor, but I don't really know any sailors, so I couldn't tell you that. It was what some would call 'colorful' language at any rate.

Glimmer and Little Al were having a field day, mocking the brute. They rose to their feet and were beeping and whirring all kinds of things. Molly looked as if she would be blushing, if she could, indeed, blush.

The last coherent thing Dim heard was, "We'll burn it to the ground!"

Of course, there were a few other choice words in there, but that was the gist. The two passed Dim's motley crew on the way out. The brute laughed at them as they passed by, but the slender one just looked at her and smiled.

"Dim, my lovely, it's been too long!" The woman said and hugged her, a bit too strong for the gnome. Her face glowed as if she had not just been screaming bloody murder at Mallory's two henchmen just a few minutes ago. Dim returned the hug in kind, though. It had been too long, and the woman reminded her, fondly, of her parents. Even her smell was much like them.

"How have you been managing, since your... Forget those pleasantries, come in. It's nice to be visited by someone I actually want to see." She gave a menacing look towards where the henchmen had gone and pulled Dim inside.

Bor laid down and napped where he stopped. Glimmer hesitated at the door, her head lowered, eyes to the floor. The other two stood behind.

"You too, come in. All is fixed. All is forgiven." Mrs. Appleby looked directly into the tinker girl's eyes. "Let's make sure it stays that way, yes?"

Glimmer nodded slowly and entered the farmhouse. Little Al stopped and looked the same as Glimmer had. "That was for all of you." The old woman said as she went to the kitchen. Molly pushed the boy inside.

"Will they really do as they said?" Dim asked.

"What? Burn the place?" Dim nodded, "Ah, maybe. But Mallory and I go back very far. Way back when we were toddlers, I guess." She seemed a bit lost in thought.

Dim took a glass of wine from her. "What were they here for?"

Mrs. Appleby was shaken from her daydream. She rose (or really lowered it) her glass to the gnome's, "You."

"Me?"

The woman went to sit and offered Dim and the tinkers chairs. The three were already off to find the treasures of the house as they had many times before. "Break nothing!" Dim yelled. "I'm really sorry about last time, Ma'am." She felt like a little kid who broke her grandmother's window with a ball.

"Shut it with that ma'am stuff, Dim. I'm not your mother." She leaned back in her chair. "They were asking about that salesman guy you've been sending around."

"Garrick?"

"Yeah, that's him. I'm not sure I like him." She thought a minute, "He's a great salesman, don't get me wrong, that's why I'm not sure I like him." She laughed hard and then went into a coughing fit that lasted way too long for Dim's liking.

"That's it? My little company makes them threaten you?" Dim asked after the coughing subsided. Her eyes got big. She was extremely surprised anyone would threaten the Appleby farm in this village.

"Little company?" The woman looked at Dim, looking to see if she was serious. She decided she was. "Little girl, they are afraid of your 'little company.' What you have would save us tons of man hours. They wouldn't waste the time to even come here if they weren't scared of you taking over."

Dim didn't know if she should be happy or downright terrified. She decided to be terrappy, or maybe happified. She wasn't sure which, but definitely one of those. "Did you want me to show you one of the tools? Maybe you could try one?"

"Oh no, your salesman, Garrick, you said, already demonstrated." She rubbed her chin and cleared her throat loudly. "How much 'magic' is in these things? I don't trust it much."

The gnome felt in her pocket. The feeling of the box in her hand eased her anxieties and doubt. She had been keeping it on her more and more, she noticed, feeling almost naked without it. Sometimes the anxiety was merely a feeling that it had fallen out. She drew a breath and looked at her friend directly in the eyes. This was the moment she needed. This was the moment to sell. "Not much, it just keeps the gears wound. Ninety-nine percent is just my gadgetry."

Mrs. Appleby glimpsed at the gnome's pocket, then let out a huge laugh. "As long as I have a warranty. The self-stirring pot almost took down the house."

"Of course, I'll fix anything."

"I think the Reaperator 250 or something like that, I could use a bunch of those for the fall. Also, that tiller thing, we'll need them soon though. Maybe six to start."

"3000."

"Excuse me, dear."

"Nothing. Garrick said that you were definitely out, though. Why are you buying now?"

"Nothing against your Garrick, deary, but he is a salesman. Can't trust them. You are family. I trust your word." She looked at Dim's pocket again, then off to the wall. Some memory was there, but she was not about to share it. "And I'm sick of Mallory thinking she has something on me."

Dim stayed and visited a while until Glimmer came in with a very guilty look on her face. The gnome decide that it was time for a hasty retreat. Besides, Mrs. Appleby was coughing more and still refusing to tell her what was wrong. She also looked extremely tired.

"Bring up those tillers as soon as you can," Mrs. Appleby said between a cough and an enormous yawn.

"I'll send them tomorrow." She yelled.

"Use the elf girl and the big one. I like them." She turned to go inside, but stopped. "Not the Garrick and definitely not the magic guy."

Dim gave a thumbs up as they slowly rode out, Bor pulling them along incredibly slowly. She'd have to look at him. Glimmer and Little Al were waving to the old woman with a bit too much vigor, and Little Al couldn't help himself but giggle. "What did you three do?"

Little Al and Glimmer pointed directly at Molly, who stood there expressionless. If she did not know better, Dim would have said that she blushed this time.

Chapter 11

Little Thief

It was early afternoon as they moved through the center of town. Dim's stomach was rumbly, and she thought about what she had to eat at home. There wasn't much. And there was even less of what she would want to eat.

She thought to stop at the tavern when she saw Earch and Garrick sneaking towards its window. They were trying to be stealthy, but with Earch there, that would never happen.

Something was up.

Dim jumped off the wagon, which was nearly stopped with Bor's glacial pace anyway, and told the ox to bring the tinkers back home. Glimmer looked distraught to not get an invitation and whirred her disapproval at the gnome.

"I'm not sure what's going on, and I'm hungry. You don't have the patience for either of those things." Dim said to her and then turned to Little Al, "Don't forget to feed the... cat-thingy?" She said and scrunched her

face. She really needed to give it a name if it was staying. Just calling it the... cat-thing? and scrunching her
face, as she did every time, was not a good name.

Glimmer pouted and crossed her arms as Little Al
nodded affirmative. Molly was still sitting with a blank
stare. Dim wondered what it was she had done, but figured she'd find out, eventually. Right now, she wanted
to find out what the boys were doing.

The gnome snuck behind the two. Well, one really,
Garrick was almost impossible to sneak up on. Earch,
on the other hand, was still talking as Dim reached him.

"I can not understand what she is doing with her."
He said as he turned to see Dim had joined them. He
shot Garrick a look that Dim took as a 'what is she doing here?' look. Dim returned a glare to him.

"Who is doing with who?" She said.

Earch stepped away from the window and tried to
walk by them, "Um... You with Mrs. Appleby, of
course."

She wasn't buying it, but played along a bit, "Selling
things."

"How did it go, hon?" Garrick asked.

"Great, six tillers by tomorrow."

"I'll bring them over with Bromm then."

Dim reach out and grabbed Earch's arm as he tried
to walk away. "No, she doesn't like you. Bromm and Zaela will need to bring them."

Earch stopped. "I am not sure about Zaela. I can go."
Garrick hit him.

"She doesn't like me? Everyone likes me." Garrick looked hurt.

"Not you personally. She doesn't like salesmen." Dim then turned to Earch, "You she just doesn't like." She lied a little. Mrs. Appleby just seemed to not trust magic, but Earch just lied to her, so she felt it was okay. "I'll go if she can't, but why can't she?"

Garrick pointed to the window. Dim took a peek inside. The elf was sitting with Mallory's hench-woman having a drink and touching her arm. She seemed to hang on every word the woman said.

"What is she doing with her?" Dim asked.

"That's what I asked?" Earch responded.

"But, apparently, that was about me." She shot him a look. She felt something in the pit of her stomach. A pang she had never felt before. It made her feel sick. Was she jealous, or did she feel betrayed? She wasn't sure. She really had not felt this in all her life. "I'm going in."

"I do not think that's a good idea, Dim." Earch grabbed her arm this time to stop her. She shook him off and looked at Garrick. He nodded that he agreed.

"She already knows that you're here, and probably me, too."

"We've been quite quiet." Garrick said.

Dim looked over at Earch and scoffed. Garrick gave a look as if to say, yeah, you're right. "It's Zaela. She probably knew you were following her the moment you started. Might have wanted you too." She straightened her dress. "She's in the tavern. Obviously, she's not hiding. And I'm hungry."

Firmly gripping the box in her pocket, which seemed to her to be humming slightly, almost happily, Dim made her way inside and took a table across the room. The boys followed. They had to see what happened next.

The three of them sat by the door. Not their normal table, seeing that Zaela and her 'friend' were too close to that for comfort. Dim ordered her usual, a shaved steak sandwich on a long split oval bun with onions and a fine goat's cheese melted over it. It was, normally, a glorious sandwich that came with some sliced potatoes that were boiled in a garlic oil before being coated with sea salt and ground up black pepper seeds. Her mouth would water with anticipation of the presentation of the sandwich. It was one of her greatest pleasures. It was gigantic. To a normal sized human woman, it could be split into three meals easily. For a tiny gnome, four or five.

For this particular tiny gnome, two-ish.Today, she might as well have just ordered the gruel. The sloshy, oaty, tasteless gunk that was normally given away to those who needed a meal after spending all their money on booze. She did not enjoy a single bite.

Her head was spinning. She was more than just a bit mad, and she now understood why they called it 'mad.' She was absolutely infuriated. Dim had never felt this way before in her life, and she could not control it.

She tried to pick up her wine and take a sip. Perhaps that would calm her. But when she looked at her hand, it was shaking uncontrollably. It did not even seem to be part of her body. She decided to forgo the wine and reached into her pocket. For the briefest instant, she feared the box was gone. She fumbled and found it. The humming, which she thought everyone in the tavern should be able to hear, soothed her. No one looked in her direction besides the boys, who were talking to and looking very concerned towards her, so she felt safe that no one else could hear it.

The gnome did hear the words coming from Earch and Garrick, but none of them registered in her brain. She attempted to smile and nod, something her father had told her to do when she wasn't really paying attention to something, but wanted to look like she did, but the looks on their faces seemed to suggest that she was not nodding or smiling at the right times. Or the right way.

Her thoughts were looping. From the woman yelling "we'll be back!" and the man yelling "we'll burn it all down!" to little things like 'was there food for the cat' and 'did I turn the stove off' rambled through her head.

One thought, 'I must find Bromm to ask him to help me bring the machines to Mrs. Appleby tomorrow morning' ran through the most. Although the worst was that she wanted to punch her friend in the face for being with their enemy. One who had threatened her friend, no her 'family,' earlier in the day.

She had never, ever felt this way before.

It was more than anger. Although that was definitely there.

It was jealousy.

'That's stupid, we kissed once,' she thought. But she knew it was. Not that she wanted Zaela, it was that someone else was with her. It was also something she never thought she would ever feel since she had not felt this since she was a little girl and her mother had watched another child. She saw her mother playing with them and had pushed the child down. This was, obviously, not the same, exactly, but close. It was intense.

She gripped the box tighter, and it felt its warmth, its calm.

Her first thought was to go to her mother, which struck her deep. That ship had long sailed. Her next was Bromm.

She had to find Bromm.

Dim attempted to roll her fore and middle finger towards the owner of the tavern to get him to wrap her meal, but could not get his attention. She had to leave. Dim brought her food up to the counter and asked for a box. Earch and Garrick were with her, but she barely noticed.

She did, however, notice the woman, who had been with her 'friend,' who worked for Mallory and who had previously threatened Mrs. Appleby, come to the bar as well.

The woman said something to Dim, who really did not know what she said. She only felt a rage that she had never felt before.

She envisioned herself picking up the large mug that lay empty next to her and slamming it into the woman's face. She saw it so deeply that for a moment she thought she had actually done it, watching the slender woman bleeding, her face sheared in multiple places, lying on the floor.

The problem was not that she imagined it.

The problem was that she laughed when she did. It had felt so real, so vivid, that she felt it had happened. Maybe in a different life.

She reached into her pocket and stroked the box. The image faded from her mind. A calm rested over her. To the woman, she must have looked crazed, as she backed away quickly after getting her drinks.

Dim took her to-go box and left the tavern.

She vaguely remembered that the boys had followed her for a bit, calling out, until she saw Bromm around the corner.

"Little Thief!" Bromm said, smiling,

"Please take me home." Was all she could say to him. And, of course, he did.

The gnome was so happy that it was Bromm who walked her home. For one, Bromm would ask, 'What's the matter?' and if you said 'I don't want to talk about it.' he just said 'okay.' That was pretty much the first half of the conversation they had as they walked through the streets of the village.

He was also great if you wanted to talk. He would listen and listen and would never interrupt you, unless he needed you to clarify something, and then he would give the best and simplest advice.

But she did not want that right now. She was seeing red and would not really process anything that he said, anyway.

The other reason was that she needed him to come by in the morning to help with the deliveries to Mrs. Appleby, and this saved her from having to find him later. Not that he was ever really hard to find, but now she could just go home and go to bed.

Of course the giant would be there early, no he did not want to stay over (she asked as she always did and he declined, as he always did). Yes, he would take half of the sandwich. Thanks for asking.

Then he left.

The tinkers were about, but she paid them no mind. The same with the cat-like-thing. Hopefully, they had fed it, but she was tired and in a way she had not been before that she remembered, sad.

She changed and got into bed thinking about the deliveries in the morning, gripping the wooden box. She smiled and slept well for the first time in forever.

Bromm was there bright and early, before the sun, and woke his friend.

"I'm always surprised that you can fit through my door," she told him.

"I've learned to fit through things I probably shouldn't be able to. Nothing here, or most places, was built for my size, Little Thief." He said. There was a tinge of sadness in it.

"I know that feeling." She smiled. Dim knew that 'Little Thief' began as a rib, but it stuck. A sort of term of endearment. They had a connection beyond a love of adventuring and steak sandwiches. They were both misfits pretty much everywhere. She only ever remembered him calling her Dim once, and that was under duress, so it probably doesn't count. "I'll warm the rest of the steak and get dressed if you want to start loading."

"Already ate." He said.

"You're turning down food?" He nodded and patted his belly. 750 pounds and still watched his weight. "Tea then?"

To that inquiry, he nodded.

Dim put on her 'business' dress (which really was the one with the least rips in it and the rips it had were easy to hide. She thought that she should probably get a few more, since it was all she wore, but she hated shopping for most things. Food was okay when needed. Metal and gears and screws were a wonderful shopping experience. Anything else, not so much. She scoffed down half of her steak sandwich while the tea and coffee were still brewing, poured them into two cups with hinged tops and made her way to meet Bromm.

The giant had the wagon loaded and was ready to pull it. "Hop on."

"You're not pulling this thing, I'll get Bor."

"Bor wouldn't move. I don't mind."

She patted her own belly and gave Bromm a look to say, 'you sure?'

He let out a great laugh and turned his head to the wagon. "Alright, but if you get tired, just say the word and I'll take over."

"Maybe you pull me back." He said with another laugh. Dim smiled as they made their way along the long and winding road that she took the day before with the tinkers. She left them home after much protest, except for Molly, who still seemed embarrassed about something. Hopefully, that was nothing to worry about.

After about the halfway mark, Bromm interrupted the silence, "So what was the bother last night?"

She thought about it for a while. Obviously she thought about it too long because eventually Bromm said that it was okay if she did not want to talk about it. Eventually she let out an, "I don't know."

"I was pissed off too, you know."

"At Zaela?" she asked.

"Yeah." He could have said more like that she was dating an enemy and that it wasn't right. About how at least she should have told them she was dating her. But that was not how Bromm did things. You knew how he felt about what he said and how he said it. In this situation, he saw both sides.

"You went back?"

"Yeah."

"Did you say anything?"

"Nope."

Dim sat back. She had something else, but she did not want to say it. She knew that Bromm already knew it, but it was not quite real until it left her lips. "I was more than angry."

"Jealous." He said. It was not a question, it was a statement.

"I don't know. I've never had romantic feelings for anyone. I still don't, not even for her. But there was something. Anger, yes. Betrayal, yes. I guess jealousy as well."

"You don't have to have romantic feelings to be jealous." The giant said.

They said nothing else until they reached the house. Mrs. Appleby met them at the door and greeted Bromm with a friendly smile, hugging Dim. They had a pleasant conversation, and the deal was done.

Then all their lives changed.

Chapter 12

Why a Stag?

They made it back to Dim's house not long after noon. "Mind if I sit out back and whittle a bit?" Bromm asked.

"Of course." Dim was actually quite excited he was staying. She normally enjoyed sitting alone and tinkering around, but the big sale was a bit emotionally exhausting and she could use the silent company. "Afternoon tea and biscuits?"

"Always." He went to walk out back, then turned, "And honey?"

"I'll see what I have." She went in and rolled out the biscuits after stoking the oven. Glimmer came over and rested next to her.

"What's wrong, little one?" She asked. Then immediately regretted it.

The brass girl went on a five-minute beeping and whirring tirade about something that seemed to have to do with Little Al and the cat-like creature. Dim tried her best to follow along, but really only caught that it killed things and left them in the yard and shed constantly. Of course, Little Al did not clean it up, so she and Molly had to. This, she seemed to argue, was totally unfair, and she was now complaining, to what she referred to as management.

"So, I'm management now?" Dim asked.

Glimmer just looked at her and shrugged in a 'well, yeah' kind of way.

Dim sighed. She always thought of the tinkers as more than just well, gadgets. The gnome always hoped that they thought of her as more than just 'management,' and never really even told them to be the cleaners and fixers. She was pretty sure that was Molly. The gnome would actually be quite surprised by what each of them actually thought about her.

"I'll talk to him about it."

Glimmer huffed a bit and stormed off.

"I will!" Dim said and poured the tea. The biscuits would be a bit. The honey was a bit crystallized, but otherwise fine. She'd warm it some before serving.

As she went to bring the tea out to Bromm, the bell Zaela had installed above the door a while ago when Dim had fallen asleep and apparently three or four customers had come and went as she snored away, oblivious to this, rang. She looked over to see an older man, quite nervous by the look of him, hovering by the door.

"Come in, Mr. Davies! What can I do for you?" She asked, putting on the fake smile that Garrick had made her practice a thousand times. It still felt forced to her, but Mr. Davies seemed to perk up a bit.

"Um, I'm not totally sure." He said and came over to her.

"Some tea, maybe?" Dim asked, then remembered Garrick's 'Customer Service 101' class he made her go through. She had wanted to ask what the 101 was for, but had realized he would just say something like 'numbers make it sound better' or something like that, so she never did. She remembered to add a "Mr. Davies." after her question, though. Saying the customer's name as much as possible seemed to be a big thing in sales.

"If you don't mind, yes."

"I have biscuits baking, but they'll be awhile, if you want to wait."

"No, thank you. I must get back soon." He looked out towards the door as if someone may have followed him.

Dim brought out Bromm's tea and gave one to Mr. Davies. "Well, how can I help you?" She asked, hoping it would be quick. She wanted to sit in silence with Bromm before the biscuits were done.

"Yes, well." He looked to the door again, then continued quietly, "I saw what you brought Mrs. Appleby, and was kind of thinking that, maybe..."

"You want one?" She asked. Very surprised and very excited.

He almost reached across to shush her, but restrained himself. "Yes." then added, "Maybe two." He hesitated and then continued, "One for now, see what happens."

Dim held in her excitement. He was skittish, probably because of Mallory, and that woman who was with Zaela's doing. She understood his nervousness now, and why he kept looking at the door. "I'll bring one to the farm tomorrow."

"Thank you." Mr. Davies said, took another sip of the tea and after saying "great tea." left quickly.

Dim threw out the rest and poured herself another cup. She went out and sat next to Bromm.

"Who was that?"

"Customer."

"Already?"

"Quick, huh?"

"Yep."

"Delivery tomorrow?"

"Yep." Dim looked at what he was carving. "What's that?"

"Stag."

"Why?"

"Why?" Bromm looked at her with a look of shock. Well, as close to shock as she had ever seen from him. "The stag is one of my people's most powerful symbols." Figuring that was the end of the conversation, Bromm went back to whittling.

Dim didn't want to break the silence. It was kind of their thing. They finished their tea, and she poured more. She took the biscuits out and served them with the warmed honey that was absolutely delicious. She had to remember how she made them. 'I really should write these things down once in a while,' she thought to herself. The gnome was trying to remember how much of everything she had put in the mix, but she usually just threw the ingredients in without measuring. After a while she gave up, or, in reality, got bored with thinking about it.

"But why?" she asked.

"Why what?" It had been about a half hour since they had talked about it, so he did not realize what she was talking about.

"Why a stag?"

"Ah, it's the symbol of my hometown's patron." He watched as Glimmer came over and sat down cross-legged, anticipating a story. She always knew when a story was about to be told and would never be out of earshot if one was to be told. Little Al peeked around the corner to see what was happening as well. "Also, of my Glencing team." He looked proud at the team's mention.

"What's Glencing?" Dim said, then retracted, "Wait, no, maybe later. Tell me more about your patron. I didn't even know you had a patron."

Bromm's face fell from proud down into a quiet, depressed concentration. For a moment, Dim and Glimmer and even Little Al thought that the giant would not continue. But with a sigh after a few minutes, he began.

"The elders told us of them. Of Skovfyr. The Moon. The night. And of his twin, Solfrid. The day. The Sun. Our town, being mainly hunters, always worshiped Skovfyr mainly. Although, with him, must come Solfrid as well. As time went on, they said, the women became the chosen ones of Solfrid as the men became the chosen of Skovfyr."

"The men and women worship different gods?"

"In a way, although we worship both." Bromm looked at the gnome. "Don't your people have many gods?"

Dim looked to her feet. "I don't know my people. The only one I've ever met, I'm not sure really existed."

Bromm looked at her with a bit of pity, which she despised, but also with understanding. She wondered why they had never talked about any of this before, but realized that their silence was part of their bonding.

Bromm continued, "The two were locked in an eternal hunt. Skovfyr would chase Solfrid through the day and many times roam, lost, throughout the night. Looking for his twin, his mate." Glimmer and Little Al made faces at each other in this revelation. Dim gave them a dirty look, and they regained their composure. Bromm did not seem to notice this interaction. "The hunter was destined to spend eternity hunting a prey that he could never conquer."

"Did he ever catch her?"

"From time to time. The first time he caught her, the Chaos God, Morkvedr, Ruler of the Hells, was trying to spread chaos upon the land. The twins were locked in a great battle as they led their combined armies against his. But all seemed lost. Morkvedr's armies came from the breaches in the dimensions, and soon all of my people, and our gods' armies, were overrun with the daemons."

Glimmer made some whirs and motioned to Dim. "What's she want?" Bromm asked the gnome.

"She doesn't know what a Daemon is."

"Ah, yes. They are from the Hells. Agents of Chaos. They are in a war with what we call the Muses, the agents of order."

Glimmer put her hands out like a scale. Little Al mimicked her and laughed. The woman tinker chased him away.

"So the Daemons are evil and the Muse's are good?" Dim asked, after settling the two tinkers down.

Bromm laughed. "Not at all. Good and evil are not the same as chaos and order. Many of the muses are quite evil. The Vapryr, for example." He shook his head. "Just stay clear of the Vapryr. They're no good." He laughed a bit, but not a jolly, good-natured laugh. There was another story behind that laugh, but not for today. Before Bromm could get back to his story, the bell to the door rang out.

Dim walked into her house to see who was there. Glimmer and Little Al sat staring at the giant, waiting for him to finish his tale.She would regret later not staying with the giant and hearing his story.

Bromm looked down at the little tinkers; especially Little Al, who seemed all so eager to hear whatever it was that the giant was going to tell Dim about the stag. He waited, hoping that the metal constructs would wander away at some point. They did not. He also found that his tea was empty and that Little Thief was quite occupied inside her store. He sighed, looked at the tinkers, and told them a different tale, one of Stefnir Vintr; or as he is more well-known as, Father Mid-Winter.

Chapter 13

From Bad to Worse to... Worser? Worstest?

It turned out that the farmers were waiting for one person, one big farm, to take the chance. Once Mrs. Appleby put in her order, almost every other farmer was on board. There were a few holdouts. Either they were happy with Madame Mallory's products or in fear for their farms, but the majority came in that day to place orders.

As the weeks went on, Dim's Enchanted Yard and Farm Tool Company overtook Madame Mallory's empire as the largest tool supplier in the village. Now Mallory certainly had more power, as this was just a small branch of her empire. But the takeover was swift. The farmers were just waiting for an alternative and when it came; they ditched Mallory without a thought.

This was when Mallory was not around.

A few weeks in, Dim's bell rang a bit after closing hours. Although this was not too unusual, the gnome was welcoming if a customer had a question, comment, complaint, or concern. She'd known most of these people, though not well, all of her life. And they had, for the most part, always welcomed her, even with her differences, so it seemed only fair to return the favor.

This night, the visitor was not a welcomed one, however, as Esus entered her store and home. Dim wished that she had taken Garrick's advice about locking the place, now that she had things to steal. She had never locked it before. She was not even sure if her locks still worked.

She watched from the other room as she sifted through her workshop area. "I'll be with you in a moment." She called out, hopefully with some confidence. Glimmer looked at her with concern as Little Al and Molly tried to secure some sort of weapon. "Take your time. I'm just browsing." The woman said. "Oops!" Then there was a crash. Nothing horribly bad, but it made a point.

Dim pushed her hands down to calm the tinkers, but then grabbed her knives she used when adventuring. She looked at them for a moment. She kind of had thought that she would not need them again. That seemed a stupid thought now.

Another thing clattered to the floor. "Oops, I'm so clumsy!" The woman laughed.

Dim strapped the knives on and reached into her pocket, caressing the box. She closed her eyes and felt the anxiety leave her and enter it. It hummed again happily.She walked out to meet Mallory's hench-woman, and apparently Zaela's girlfriend, with a calm smile on her face. "Oh, pay no mind to that." the gnome spoke calmly with what she has hoping was not a dumb-looking smile on her face, "What brings you all the way out here so late?"

"Just a fine night for a stroll." This was absolutely true. Dim was thinking of walking over to the tavern herself for dinner just a few minutes before her visitor came.

"What can I help you with?"

The slender one eyed where Dim's knives caused a slight bump under her dress. She held up her hands. "No need for aggression, I am merely a messenger," Esus said.

"I do have operating hours."

"We thought that you may not want customers to hear this." She replied, "Although they will know soon enough as well."

"So, what is this message, then?"

"Mallory is not happy."

"Why is that my problem? It seems like that should concern you more than me."

"Exactly why it is your problem as well."

"I don't follow."

"My problems are your problems," she said.

"Mallory demands results." She walked to the door. "And I am the one who must deliver those results."

Dim followed her to the door and pushed it closed behind Esus. She turned the lock for the first time in years. She let out a deep sigh as she heard the click.

She sank down to the floor, thoughts racing through her head. Glimmer came over to her with her head down. She pulled the tinker close and hugged her. Little Al and Molly soon followed. They stayed that way for quite some time.

Mallory did indeed come back. She met with many of the farmers and although a few stopped using Dim's Enchanted Yard and Farm Tool Company, many continued to. Business actually picked up as the minors and loggers started coming in and asking if Dim could create specialized tools for them as well.As the weeks went on, Dim and Earch worked closely together, building the tools. They began to joke and needle each other like before. Garrick took over most of Zaela's delivery duties as she spent more and more time with Esus, eventually moving in with her.

This did not go over well with Dim, but alas, there was not much she could do about it. And since Garrick did not really need to sell as much as find out what exactly the customers wanted, he was fine with it. Bromm, as usual, did the heavy lifting.

One thing that picked up was complaints.

It was slow at first, just a couple of problems that were fixed with tweaks or tinkers. Some really were just that the customer wanted more power or a modified feature. Nothing big, easy fixes.

Then there were some break-downs.

These irked Dim. Not to mention Garrick. She was used to having breakdowns with her small gadgets before, but since the snow-flinger, nothing really had gone wrong.Not since the box. Since the box, she had been able to concentrate on the design of the machines and not all the details to power them. With that out of the way, she concentrated on the quality and, she would admit, her creativity. The gnome felt that, since acquiring the box, her creativity had increased significantly.

What was breaking on the machines made little sense.

For example, in the +2 Loggerator that they sold a week prior had a rod bend and then break clean off. She had been getting the rods from the same vendor since she was ten and never had one break. It was an easy fix, but cost the loggers a few hours of work.

Today Mr. Davies came in.

"How can I help you," Dim said, then added, "Mr. Davies?" It still felt so weird saying the name of someone she had known for so long.

"I tried the Reaperator 3000 yesterday, just to test, you know. Get ready for the Autumn and it was making a..." He seemed to either be clearing his throat or making a noise that the Reaperator 3000 was making. Dim turned her head slightly.

Mr. Davies looked at her, realized that his point was not being made, and tried again. "It's going kind of 'whir, whir, bang.'"

"Whir, whir, bang?"

"Whir, whir, bang, yes." He looked at her again, then at the floor. "Sometimes there's another bang."

"I'll have to have a look. Can I come up this afternoon?"

"I'm sure it's nothing. I just want to be ready for the season."

"No problem, Mr. Davies. I'll be out and get you squared away today. I just have one appointment and then I'll be there."

"Thank you, Dim. This is why I wanted to go with you. Service is great." He smiled and left.

Glimmer sat next to her on the desk. She held up her hand.

"I know, five today. You know you only have four fingers, though, right?"

Glimmer gave her a look to say, 'get serious!' Then pretended to hold her non-existent nose.

"Yes, something smells fishy." She went to get her tool bag. "I still need to fix it though. I hope this isn't what I'm going to be doing all the time now. Fixing things."

Glimmer shrugged in a 'looks that way' kind of way.

"Had more fun making gadgets that exploded." She mumbled as she left the room. Glimmer agreed.

Dim and Glimmer got to Mr. Davies' farm around two. She found the problem around two and fifteen. Another rod.

But this one had not broken yet. Oh, it was bent and close to coming apart, but still intact.

Someone had also sawed it through to a point that it would break quickly. Had she been so stupid and not seen what was going on, or was this one just done quick and sloppy-like? That she did not know. She did, however, know who was doing it.

And it was time to confront them.

"Let's go, Glimmer." She said, taking the rod with her.

"Is it fixed?" Mr. Davies yelled from the house as he saw her leaving.

"Give me a day." She replied. Dim was in no mood, but felt that she sounded rude. She stopped and turned to him. "I just need to get a part."

Mr. Davies waved and went inside.

Dim reached into her pocket and felt the box. It did not calm her, but heightened her anger. She rubbed it more as she made her way to Zaela's new house.

Earch saw her on the way. He knew that look. He had only seen it a few times, but his friend was about to explode.

"Slow down. Where are you going?" He looked at her and then at the rod. "And why do you have a metal stick?"

"They've been sabotaging us."

"Who?"

That stopped her. She looked at him as if he could not possibly be that stupid. This was a look that he had never seen before.

"Okay, but where are you going?"

"Just paying our 'friend' a visit."

"You do not really think that Zaela had anything to do with this, do you?"

"Maybe not. But she certainly hasn't been around at all."

"That is ridiculous, Dim. Let us sit and calm down."

Her nostrils flared, her breathing heavied. She was redder than the reddest she had ever been. "I. Am. Calm."

Earch stepped back as the gnome continued. He recovered quickly. "Maybe give me the box, at least."

She rubbed it again. "It's the only thing keeping me calm." She would look back at this statement at the end of the day and realize that was a lie, and she knew it when she said it. At that moment, however, she felt that she believed it.

Earch followed her to Zaela's new apartment. He climbed the stairs behind her and Dim banged on the door with the rod. "What is wrong with you?" Zaela asked.The elf looked out at the beady eyed, red-faced gnome. She stepped back as she saw the look on her face.Dim wanted to say quite a few things, but the anger was peaking when she saw the elf's face, mistaking Zaela's fear with guilt. "Sabotage!" was the only word that came out as she pushed into the apartment, holding up the rod.

"You!" she yelled at Esus from across the room. She would have run towards her with the rod if it were not for the combined effort of Earch and Zaela, and to a much lesser degree Glimmer, who was almost, but not quite, as hot as Dim.

The rod struck Zaela above her eye.Esus pulled one of her knives and went towards the gnome. Earch moved between them and took a slice from the knife to his hand. A minor wound and nothing that would not heal, but it hurt badly.

"You do not come into my house like this," Esus yelled.

"Like you have come into mine?" Dim retorted.

"Like what?" Zaela said, recovering.

"She came threatening this very thing a few weeks back, threatening me."

"I did not threaten you."

"Seemed like it to me, and you broke my stuff."

"I merely dropped a few things," going to Zaela, who pushed her away slightly. "Just an intimidation technique."

Dim looked at her. She was not calming. She rubbed the box again; it heightened her rage.. She started towards the woman, but again Earch, who was actually bleeding pretty good now, and Zaela, who seemed concussed, held her.

"You are evil!" She screamed, but no one really understood what she said. The box was absolutely humming and glowing at the exchange. Earch tried to take it from her pocket. She fought this, but he succeeded eventually.

"You all think I'm crazy, but she and her boss are sabotaging us." She turned to Zaela. "And you, worst of all, have turned on me."

She pushed her way past the two and went home, Glimmer in tow, after the tinker made a rather crude gesture at Esus. Without the box, she felt naked. She kept reaching for it and became more and more agitated each time it was not there.

She cursed Esus again as she tried to open the door, realizing she had locked it. This was not what she wanted. She wanted her friends back. She wanted to feel safe, and she wanted to not have to lock her damned door!

After fumbling for her keys and entering, Dim slammed the door, without her knowledge, in Glimmer's face and fell onto her bed. She thought to lock the door and looked up, only to see the shocked face on Glimmer. The gnome motioned the tinker to her and gave her a hug, pulling her onto the bed.

"We'll just stay here. Forget everything else and stay here." She said over and over, hugging the girl. Finally, she fell asleep.

Later that day, Bromm knocked on the door.

"I'm not doing anything today!"

"It's night."

"I'm not doing anything tonight, then!"

Bromm stopped for a moment. "You'll have to."

"Why?"

"Mrs. Appleby's farm is on fire."

Chapter 14

Lifeless

Dim jumped from her bed and ran to the door, actually pushing Bromm aside. The giant did not know that the gnome had that much strength and actually staggered. Unnoticeable to anyone, but he felt his balance sway the tiniest bit. She impressed him.

Looking towards the farm, she saw the smoke. Impressive from how far away they were. This was big. Too big to wait.

"Can you get me there?" She turned to him. She hated being carried, and Bromm knew it. It was embarrassing, but there were a few times that she asked him. The sheep revolt, for one, during the stampede. She needed his size, and he had obliged then, as he did now. He scooped her without a word and was running full speed.

Oh, and Bromm could run. Almost as fast as the fastest of horses in full sprint. It was a sight to behold when he needed speed.

Some of the village folk had come into the street as the smell of smoke filled the air. It was too far for them to know exactly where it was coming from, but just based on the size of the cloud and the direction, they knew. Dim yelled for them to help, and many did. The tavern owner came running first. Then many others.

This was a devastation to all. If Mrs. Appleby's farm went up, food would be scarce for the second winter in a row.

Beyond that, everyone liked the woman.

She would help you out without you asking. She just knew that you needed a hand. No one understood how she knew, but prices would suddenly drop the instant you had trouble paying. And right before you said that you couldn't pay. Never once would she out and out give you something, but she found a way to get it to you without you having to ask and humble yourself. She knew pride.

Mrs. Appleby knew the village and took care of it.

Now Mrs. Appleby needed the village, and the village would be there for her instead.

It was not quite too late when everyone got there to help, but it was late enough. And the fires, the fires were unnatural. Some kind of magic to them.

Earch took heat from some for that. He was, after all, the only mage (at least that anyone knew of) around. Whispers, and more than whispers, fled the village for years about the mage fire and how Earch had started it. In some tales, it was accidental, but some blamed him outright.

It was unfair, but so was life, it seemed.

Bromm and Dim reached the farm before most, but there were a few there fighting the fire already. Mallory, Esus and Zaela among them. Dim gave them a look, but did not linger. There was work to do.

Earch was also there with Garrick.

To everyone's credit, they all were attempting to dull the flames. Fortunately for Mrs. Appleby's house, but maybe unfortunately for Earch himself, his water spells seemed very effective against the flames. This probably helped to fuel the speculation that he had something to do with starting it.

Water, however, seemed stunted against the mystical flames. It did the job, eventually putting it out, but it should have doused it quicker.

In the end, her house was blackened, but not destroyed. It was quite intact, actually, once you got the smell of smoke out, but the farm and crops were another story. And many of the animals were either killed or too injured and had to be put down. Others had run off and took months for the herders to get them all back.

The year, at least for Mrs. Appleby, was ruined. This spelt, well, not quite disaster yet for the village, but if anything else went wrong, it certainly could. It would be a light winter, either way.

There was only one person, in Dim's mind, who benefited from this. If it was not her, it would had have to have been someone under her. That scared Dim more than if the woman had set the fires herself.

The woman who fought the fire right next to her. Madame Mallory.

Eventually, the enchanted flames subsided, and the villagers dispersed. The last ones to leave were Bromm, Dim, Earch, Garrick, Zaela, Esus, Mallory, and, of course, Mrs. Appleby. The matriarch invited them all inside for a drink.

The smell of burnt wood, animals and crops still rung in their noses as they sat around the dining table. Mrs. Appleby, who lost almost everything that day, was quite composed and poured drinks for all. She even made a tea for Bromm, knowing that he (and Dim had no idea how she knew, even to this day) did not drink alcohol.

Dim sat across from Mallory. They stared at each other.

There was small talk, but it was awkward. Finally, Dim said to Mallory, "You set this up."

"It was enchanted. I am no spell caster." She spread her hands to show no cards and nodded towards Earch.

"I am quite sure that he had nothing to do with this." Dim did not even look in his direction. "You were the one jealous of our company."

"Jealous?" Mallory said with a long drawl. She took out some tobacco and filled her pipe, taking her time.

She put it to her mouth and drew in as Esus held a match. "I am..."

Mrs. Appleby cut her off. "Now is not the time for this petty back and forth." She refilled first Dim's and then Mallory's wine, then everyone else's. "I don't think anyone here is responsible." She looked at them both. "If I did, you would not be here."

Mallory opened her mouth to speak, but Mrs. Appleby cut her off again. "I know you Mal. I have known you for quite some time. All my life even, if we're being honest. If this were someone else's farm, I may even suspect you. But not mine. You would not do this to me."

Dim watched Mallory's eyes. She wished that she had her box. She kept reaching into her dress pocket, looking for it, even though she knew it was not there. It would have told her whether Madame Mallory was lying, she was sure of it. Dim watched the woman's head lower a slight bit. It looked to her that she was, for the briefest of seconds, beaten. It wasn't her.

But then who?

Certainly not Earch, even though that concept kept coming up. Esus was with Zaela apparently, unless she was covering for her. The gnome didn't think that the elf was that far gone at this point. Not Bromm. He came to get her, and why would he? The rest of the farmers respected Mrs. Appleby way too much.

Then it hit her.

Mormoth. The brute.

"Where's your other henchman?" She asked Mallory.

"My what, dear?"

"Don't dear me. Your brute. The other one that is usually with her." Dim pointed to Esus. Zaela obviously took offense, but held her tongue for a moment. It was a good question.

"I do not know. I haven't seen him in quite a while."

"I didn't see him." Dim said, "Did any of you?"

No one could say that they did. Around the room, they all shook their heads.

"Earch, where's the box?"

Earch did not answer right away. "The damned box! Where did you put it?" She was yelling now.

"In the spot," the mage said.

"At my house?"

He nodded. Everyone rose from the table. "The tinkers." Dim thought and maybe said. It was all she could think of. Well, that and the box. The box was constantly on her mind. Maybe it was deep down in her sub conscience, but it was always there. Somewhere.

"Bromm, please." She said, with tears streaming from her face. No more needed to be said to the giant. He picked his friend up and ran to her house.

Bromm never slowed. Even at his great fatigue from the earlier sprint to Dim's house, to Mrs. Appleby's farm, fighting the fire and then this sprint back to Dim's house, he ran faster than Dim had ever seen. Even Bromm could not remember if he had run faster.

Even before they had reached the house, terror struck deep into Dim.

Though it was not lit, they could tell the sign had been broken and swinging in two pieces at the door. A fire was burning inside. Not strong, not to cause damage, but there.And there was something nailed to the door.

Not something, she saw as she got closer. Someone.

Glimmer was nailed straight through where her heart would be if she had one.

She hung there.

Lifeless.

Bromm pulled the spike from Glimmer. He pulled the metal figure down and handed her lifeless body to Dim. He knew that there was nothing that he could do for the tinker, but felt a rage he had never truly felt before. Oh, he had obviously felt rage before, but nothing like this. Glimmer may have been but a tinker toy to most. Maybe just a pet or something like that. But to him, she had been a friend.

Maybe not in the traditional way, but he had always liked that one a little more than the other two. And definitely more than almost all the people he had ever encountered in his life.

He loved when she came along on their adventures. Brave. Tireless. Knew how to handle herself and help others. Always entertaining at the campfires. The brass girl told the best stories. Bromm may have not understood a single beep or whir she made, but loved when she acted out each battle with great emphasis on how well she had done.

Even if she lied about her own deeds. That may have been the funniest parts.

Bromm hoped that the gnome could bring her back. He was not sure that she could, though. The tinker was just gears and metal and bolts physically. But she was more than those pieces when combined.

He went into the house to put out the fire. It was also mystical and took a bit of work, but he eventually got it without too much damage.

Dim, for the first time since she first touched it, did not long for the box. She would look back upon this moment later and wonder how she had let that thing take such control over her. Now was not the time, though.

Glimmer needed her.

She brought the girl into her workshop and righted her work table. Someone was in here looking for something, the box obviously, and was not gentle in doing so. He had done as much damage as possible in securing it. Dim hoped that Molly, Little Al, Bor and even the cat-like-thing were okay, but she had no time to worry about them now. She would deal with any other problems if they came up.

First, she had to try to fix... had to fix, her girl. She was the second that she ever built, and she modeled Glimmer after herself. It was like saving a part of her. Maybe a part that was long gone and could not be brought back. She was seeing how life did that recently. Took a part of you and teased you by flaunting it in front of your face, giving you hope that all could be the way it was. Some of it may be restored part of the way, but it always changed. That may, indeed, be a good thing in the long run. It almost never felt that it was a good thing at the moment, though.

If someone had ever asked her if Glimmer was her favorite of the tinkers, she would be lying if she had said no. The other tinkers knew this and never complained. She did not play favorites, and they all loved Dim in their own way.

Careful to ensure everything was perfect, she replaced what had been broken before trying anything.

The cat-like-thing came in, its hindquarters raised and ready to attack. As it relaxed, Little Al and Molly came next, their heads slung low. They would recount what had happened later, saying how heroic Glimmer was and how she had saved them. They would even mime how she saved the cat-like-thing by tricking it and making it go outside. How she had stood up to the large man and was beaten and tortured for the effort, but never gave up where the box was.

How she had battled and even struck the man, injuring his eye in the battle, before being thrown across the room and broken by the hearth. She still tried to fight.

The boy and Molly said how they wanted to fight as well, but how Glimmer had told them to stay back.

They knew she was right and that they would be broken as well. But they felt as if they were cowards. They ran. The cat-like-thing took them far away until they felt safe.

They hid until they saw the flames emerge from the house, and still they hid. They felt shame that they did not come back sooner.

Eventually, the tinkers and the cat-like-thing came back and saw her hanging upon the door, lifeless. They had tried to take her down, but could not. Tried to put out the fire, but could not, trying everything that they could think of, but nothing worked. Hope failed them.

They heard someone coming and hid. They thought that the bad man was back.

Then they saw Bromm, the Giant Man and Dim, The Creator and they hoped. Hope that their sister may still be saved.

Chapter 15

Glimmer Down

Molly and Little Al gathered around the 'operating table' as Dim went to work. She did not think that she could bring the girl, her girl, back exactly as she was, but she had to try. She was oblivious when the rest of the party from Mrs. Appleby's house, except for Mrs. Appleby herself, showed up.

Even Esus and Madame Mallory came. She did not know if this was a trick to throw her off blaming them, but she also did not care at that moment.

Earch touched her shoulders from behind, and she relaxed into him for a moment. This was something that she missed, even if it was not the romantic relationship that he longed for. Dim wanted someone that she could count on and could relax her, even at the worst of times.

Maybe she had to compromise. Let him in and see what happened. The gnome felt that this may be dishonest, leading him on. Maybe she could tell him this and see if he wanted to try it. She was not sure that it would be a good idea, however.

Although she thought about these feelings as he hugged her, she could not dwell upon it at this moment. Right now, she was trying to save her daughter.

She did all she could and put her hands on the girl's chest, hoping beyond hope that she would wake. That she would wake and be the same as she was. Then she heard him. Earch was chanting. She had heard this chant before, back when Glimmer was first made. Dim's mother had chanted it then. A bit. She could not believe that she had not remembered the chant until now.

It was words, but none she knew. It surprised her that Earch knew them.

~

Many said that Glimmer was brave. She was not in her own mind.

She did what she thought was right and what would save her friends and family.

To her own self and to her own needs, she always felt the coward. She did not stand up for herself, even to Molly, when she had said mean things to her. She let it go in favor of letting her sister feel relieved and safe. Even to the boy, who at times she felt she should shun, but he needed protection. And she was his stag, as Bromm would say.

Even if Molly thought that she was.

When the man entered their home, the others needed protection. She rushed the cat-thing outside.

It would attack the man and he would kill it instantly. Besides that, there would be blood that she felt that she would have to clean. Molly did not like blood at all. This is why she had to clean all the animals the cat-like thing brought home.

Even beyond that, the cat had saved them. It had helped them carry Little Al. It was now family until it decided to leave. She knew that if it had attacked the man, it would be broken, dead. She couldn't have that on her conscience.

She would have run herself if she saw that as an option. But the man had seen them. And she felt that he would chase them. With Little Al's track record of getting turned around, Glimmer could not risk it. As the others turn to look for her, she shut the door on them. She told them to run for it in her most grave beeps she could muster.

They did. She was happy about that.

If she were to be broken, and she was sure she was going to be, she hoped that they would be safe. Maybe the Creator could put her back together again. Maybe not.

She turned, and the man grabbed her.

~

As she worked on the girl, there was a large amount of noise behind her. She could not remember ever having this many people in her house that were not customers.

Probably never.

Her parents would, occasionally, have a large gathering in their house. She remembered hiding out in her room while they entertained until, inevitably, her mother would ask her to come out and 'be social.' Not her strong suit. She could do it if she had to, though. Her dad had trained her well.

Right now, at this instant, the people were making her want to scream.

Mostly, they were trying to help. Cleaning up the damage, salvaging what they could. They bickered a bit about who was at fault, but Dim did not care at the moment. She needed to concentrate.

The gnome blocked it out the best she could and worked. Little Al and Molly looked on with somber faces. She was replacing quite a few pieces. That did not bode well at all, thought the boy. He had thought of this before once, but with himself. How many pieces could you replace before you were now, not you?

At long last, Dim sat. She was utterly exhausted, physically, mentally, and emotionally after the day's events. She just wanted to sit and cry. Maybe have some wine. Then sleep a few days.

She turned the girl over and put the key into her back.

She turned.

Chapter 16

A Fear Gorta and a Little Lovin'

"Thank you." Dim said, as Molly brought her a glass of wine. It was not the first time that Molly had done this, but it did not happen often. The tinker was not a big fan of some of Dim's habits. She went back to watching over Glimmer with Little Al. The fallen one had yet to move.

The others had finished whatever it was they were doing and were making ready to leave. Surprisingly, the first to come to her was Mallory.

"Will it be okay?" She asked.

"I don't know if she will be yet," Dim answered with venom. "Do you really care?"

"Not particularly, but it seems important to you." She wrapped her shoulders in her cloak. "It has been a long day. If you need anything..."

"From you?"

"Yes."

Dim rose, swooned a bit from the fatigue, but caught herself. "Why on earth would you think that I would ask anything from you? For all I know, you caused this."

The woman paused and sighed. "I am ruthless in business. I would ruin your business if I thought you were a threat, and you are. Or at least, were. I don't know at this point." She turned to the gnome. "But not this way."

"Your brute threatened Mrs. Appleby before."

"That," she turned to leave, "is exactly why I fired him. Esus, a quick word." Esus walked the woman out the door. "I hope that your tinker, I think you call them, is fixed." The two women left.

The others filed out as well. Not as quick as Dim would have liked, for they all had to make the obligatory 'let me know what I can do' or 'sorry about what happened' and what not.

Earch gave her a big hug. He was the one person she would have liked to stay with her, but she couldn't ask him. She held him longer than normal. His warmth felt refreshing. He let her. Dim came close to saying 'please stay.' And he would have. But the words would not leave her mouth.

Bromm handed her the stag he had been carving. He had drilled a hole and looped it with a leather rope like a necklace. "Call to me if you ever need to."

"I will probably see you tomorrow."

He just looked at her and smiled slightly.

"Thank you, it's beautiful." He waved as he left. Dim twirled the stag in her hand as she drifted off to sleep in her chair.

She woke to a soft knock on her door and a glint of sun in her eyes through the window. She wiped spittle from her chin and turned her head from the light. To her dismay, the knock came again.

"Hells." She yelled as she knocked over the full glass of wine, which bounced and then cracked on the floor. She pulled herself up, disoriented, and went to find the broom. "What?"

A timid voice came from the other side of the door. She could tell it was Mr. Davies, even though, or maybe because he was too quiet to make out what he was saying.

Dim found the broom and made her way to the door. "What?" she said softer, but still in an annoyed manner.

"The tools you sold me are not, well, turning on."

"Did you try winding them?"

"I did. I did, yes."

"And?" she twirled her two fingers, coaxing him to continue..

"Well, they would run for a few minutes and need winding again."

"That's not good," she said, more to herself.

"No, ma'am, it isn't." Dim had never been called a 'ma'am' before. She was sure that it was out of respect, figuring that it was Mr. Davies who said it, but she did not like it one bit.

"I'll be up in a few hours, if that's okay?"

Mr. Davies nodded it was. "What happened here?" He asked, twisting his head around her to look.

Dim looked back into her house and sighed. "Not much. Someone stole my stuff, broke everything, and tried to, or maybe did, kill Glimmer, is all."

Mr. Davies' eyes grew wide. "Is all?"

"Oh yeah, they then started a fire."

"Take your time." He said and then left in a hurry.

~

"Little Thief, You made it! I wasn't sure you would come." Bromm greeted her outside the tavern. "How is the little brass girl?"

"A little better." She lied. In truth, Glimmer had yet to move that she had seen. Dim was there for, maybe, not more urgent matters, but more immediate at the least. "Is everyone here?"

"I haven't been in."

They walked in together. Well, not quite. Bromm had to turn and duck a bit to get in, so he went first. Dim followed. The crew, along with Esus, was there. Dim was not too happy about that, but it was what it was. She gave Earch a hug and nodded towards Garrick and Zaela before pulling herself up on a chair.

She sighed. "We have trouble."

"Mallory ordered us to make no more trouble with you." Esus said.

"Why does everyone fear her, then?" Dim said. She did not want to get into this now, but couldn't just say nothing.

"They fear her power. Her connections. Her money. Not violence or whatever that was yesterday."

"You came into my shop, broke stuff, and threatened me."

"To intimidate, not to actually hurt you." Her head lowered, though.

Dim took a deep breath and let it out slowly. "That's not what I'm talking about, anyway. The box..."

"Are you still obsessed with that thing?" Earch interrupted.

Dim tilted her head at him. She was too tired and too not drunk to deal with this conversation the way it was going so far. She went to the bar to cool off, retrieved a rum and some sort of fizzy syrup, something new the owner had said and wanted her to try. Spiced and sweet. She took a sip, felt the fizz tickle her throat and then ears. Smiled to him and started back.

The conversation, that had just been lively while she was away, stopped as she approached. They were probably talking about her. She probably did not look too good, having been woken early and working all day on the farms. She let it go for the moment.

"The box, as I was saying, is not working anymore."

Everyone looked at her, slightly confused.

"The tools..." she continued.

"...have stopped." Earch said. "I did not think of that."

"Yes, so all the tools..."

"All?" Garrick said.

"All." Dim said, "stopped turning on."

"Can't they just wind them?" Zaela asked.

"They can, in theory." Dim said and lowered her head. The rest looked on in anticipation. She decided it would be better to take another sip of her drink than continue. She did, then sat there. Eventually, she realized that she did, indeed, have to finish what she was saying. She mumbled it, "The winding gears are too small." Then took another quick sip.

"What?" Earch asked. She was not sure if he could not hear her or if he did not believe it.

Dim flopped her head onto the table with a thump, looked up with her hair in her face, "I made the gears small because the box kept them wound."

"Why not put the regular gears in? Just in case." Garrick asked.

"They took too long to make, demand was so high. I..."

"It was easier." Zaela interrupted.

Dim looked up at her through her disheveled hair. Tears in her eyes. She hated that she had said it, but she was not wrong. "It was easier." She admitted and covered her face in her arms.

"So, can we put gears in?" Earch tapped the table with his fingers.

"Some, maybe. Some no. It would take forever. Everything would have to be moved around for the bigger gears. And I would have to make them. It would take months just for that."

"Can't you make them go with?" Bromm asked Earch as he wiggled his fingers at him. Bromm's way of saying magic.

Earch tapped louder. "I can not. At least not permanently, like the box. There are too many tools, I would need to keep constantly casting to keep everything working. It would take all day and then I would have to start again as soon as I finished, I think." He tapped again. "If I could even could do them all in a day."

Zaela turned to Esus, "You better tell Mallory."

Dim looked up, distressed. She thought to protest. Dim did not want Mallory's help. Esus looked at Dim and waited. It was strange to see her, seemingly, waiting for Dim's permission. This was a strange dynamic. Dim wondered how she had read the woman so badly. "You should," the gnome said, finally. "The farmers need the tools."

Esus' lips curled into a slight smile. At first Dim thought it was a mocking gesture, but the slender woman touched her shoulder on the way by as she left and said. "I am sorry." Dim reached up and touched her hand before she walked away.

"So, we have two options as I see it. We fix all the tools. Which both of you have basically said we can not do." Garrick started.

"Very much not, no," Dim said, feeling the effects of her second rum and fizzy as she decided to call it.

Earch interjected that "maybe we could fix some and magic others, but," he concluded, "we would not be doing much else."

"Then, the only other option would be to pay everyone back." Zaela said.

"Yes." Garrick agreed, obviously, since he said yes.

"No good." Dim replied.

"And why?" Garrick asked.

Dim took another sip, decided that she needed food and a quick trip to the bathroom. She called over the owner, feeling that she only had enough walking balance for one trip, and ordered another rum fizzy and a steak sandwich.

"We don't have the money. A lot of it went into inventory." She intoned. It seemed as if she was spelling it out because it was obvious, but really, she just wanted to make sure that she got the words right.

"Can we, maybe, pay some back, fix some, and magic our way through a few for a while?" Zaela said as Dim hopped down, really needing the bathroom now.

"Don't know, probably not." Then she was running. The rum fizzy drink was running through her quicker than anything she had ever had. She was back in a few minutes to the same somber and quiet reaction.

She sat and sipped, waiting for something to happen. It looked like they wanted to tell her something, but it seemed no one was ready to. Their food came and then, as she put a bite into her mouth, Garrick spoke.

"Zaela has a plan."

Dim had steak and onions hanging from her mouth as she tried to speak. Feeling that speaking clearly was not happening anytime soon as she chewed her way through, she shifted the sandwich to just one hand, spilling a little, and twirled her fingers to hear more.

"I was given a map. Supposed to be big treasure," the elf said.

Dim choked a bit, swallowed, choked a bit more, then asked, "from Esus?"

"Appleby, actually." Zaela replied. "She gave it to me one day when I was delivering. Said she had no need for it and that since we were adventurers... Said that we might be able to use it. Been in her house for like ever, I guess. She said we should probably go soon."

Dim coughed a bit. The steak was stuck in her throat. She took another sip and got it down. "Why soon?"

"She didn't tell me everything, Dim, just that it has been sitting a long time. She never got around to it when she was younger."

"If Appleby gave it..." Garrick started.

"It should be good." Earch finished.

"Bromm?" Dim looked at the giant. He shrugged his shoulders, but did not look confident.

Dim took another bite of her sandwich and thought about it. "You'll go anyway, won't you?" She asked Garrick and Zaela. They both nodded.

"Can't let you go alone then."

That being settled, they spent the rest of the night eating, drinking and talking about supplies. Nothing of any significance. Zaela bowed out early to tell Esus that they would be leaving. Bromm lasted a little longer. Garrick read the room as Earch and Dim seemed to have a conversation together without him and called it a night. Truthfully, he was happy to stop being a salesman and getting back into wandering around dungeons.

Dim and Earch talked, as if it was the old times until the owner kicked them out. A night that started so downtrodden seemed to bring back a bit of what the two were missing.

Earch walked Dim home as they kept talking. They both laughed and smiled often. Then they heard it.

"Spare a bit of food, lass?" The voice came from everywhere at once, it seemed to Earch. Dim's shoulders sank. She hadn't noticed the fog. "Do you have to come every time I have food with me?"

"Who are you talking to?" Earch said.

"Him." Dim pointing into the mist. A large, slender figure appeared before their eyes.

"Who the Hells is that?"

"Fear Gorta."

"Fear, what?"

"I'll explain later." She took her leftovers out and handed it to the tall, slender man. "What is it now?" She asked.

Earch looked on in horror as the Fear Gorta devoured the food with its dagger-like teeth. Dim waited patiently as yet another of her favorite sandwiches was lost. The gnome took a moment to lament at the sacrifice they gave. She so wanted to have that in the morning and would have gone back if the owner had he not been so adamant about going home and seeing his family.

She started thinking about what food she still had at home. Maybe a few eggs and a sausage. A bit of cheese maybe. Possibly an omelet. Maybe not enough for Earch if he stayed the night. She had not quite ruled that out yet.

She watched in dismay as the Fear Gorta licked its fingers after finishing her sandwich. Maybe she would start carrying it in two containers from now on. Would it notice? She had to try. Losing this many steak and cheese sandwiches was killing her.

"Any message?" She asked as it wandered away.

"You will lose much on your journey." It said and began to fade away into the mist.

"Will the farms be saved?" Dim asked.

"Yes..." but something else he said faded into the night.

"You have met that before?" Earch asked.

"Yes."

"Is it usually correct?"

"Yes."

"Should we go?"

Dim pulled his hand and made him bend down to her. The mist faded away and a soft rain fell. She held his face in one hand and pulled him close. They kissed, truly kissed, for the first time.

Chapter 17

I Think That I Might Have Broke Him

The gnome woke early and was in a good mood for the first time since the first snow flinger had worked so many months ago.

She brewed coffee the way she knew that Earch liked it. It was strong for her, but what the Hells, she'd just brew it weaker and weaker still until he got used to it if it came to that. They had a lot to do and she could use the extra energy, anyway.

Earch watched her as she made the omelet. This is what he had always imagined they would be, but was too afraid to make it happen. He worried about what the Fear Gorta said, he had never encountered one, as Dim said she had, but the thought of 'losing much' on the journey struck him hard. Was it him? Or something else.

He got up and hugged her from behind as she cooked. She leaned back into him. He wanted this. The mage had wanted this for as long as he could remember. He did not want to lose it after the first day.

"Should we not go?" He asked, but knew what the answer was.

"I'm going," she said. He knew she would say it. "I have no choice."

"Of course you do."

"Not really. I can not let my village down. They took me in. They took Bromm in. They took Zaela in. They tolerate you."

He turned her and kissed her. "What about Garrick?" he said.

"They like his money." She laughed. The smile on her face made him feel that he would follow her into the Seven Hells.

"That thing said that you would lose much."

"We have to try to right this."

"It could mean me."

Dim put his head in her hands. A tear fell from her eye. "We have to try."

~

Our adventurers made it to the base of Mount Rune after about three days of a slogging, inconsequential journey. Dim's only trouble was having to keep telling Earch that "No, I can carry my own pack" and "I'm okay, I can get down myself" and other similar things over and over and seemingly over again. That and trying to find a way not to roll her eyes every time Garrick or Zaela gave her a look after she had to tell him these things.

On more than one occasion, she had to stop herself from just yelling at Earch. That was the toughest part, and she did not know why he was acting like this.

It was early in the evening when they reached the entrance to the cavern they sought, about suppertime, but they decided to make camp and enter during the morning after a good rest. This was not a unanimous decision. Zaela and Bromm wanted to explore immediately, so they went in for a quick look-see. Dim sat to unpack her pack and rest a bit while Bor roamed into the treeline surrounding the area.

Earch came to sit next to Dim, but this time, Garrick beat him to it.

"We're gonna need some firewood." The rogue said nonchalantly while looking at the mage.

"Yes, we will." Earch said, trying to nudge him.

"Be a dear and get some, will you? Just to get things started." The two men looked at each other, waiting for the other to flinch. "I'll help you once we start the fire."

Dim was still trying to get her bag undone. It had snagged and you know how when you are agitated and trying to get something done and it just doesn't and then you get more agitated and you just can't get the thing done and are, in fact making it worse for yourself until your are so aggravated that you give up and throw whatever it was that you were doing to the ground? That's what Dim did now.

But the bag made a noise. Not an 'I just hit the ground thumping noise,' that you would expect. No. A 'there may be someone tiny inside this bag that just hit the ground and it may have hurt,' type of sound.

The gnome picked up the bag again, got frustrated again, and almost threw the bag down again. Then she remembered that last time she did that (only a few seconds ago at this point) it made a something is in here noise, and she stopped herself. She pulled her knife and cut the drawstring.

Out popped Glimmer.

"What are you doing here?" Dim asked her.

"I was thinking the same." Garrick said to Earch, who then huffed and went to find some dry wood.

Glimmer looked annoyed, but was indeed moving about. The last Dim saw, she was immobile and had not moved since she had tried to fix her.

The brass girl mimed that she, at first, could not move, but had been able to open her eyes and hear what was going on. Then everyone kept bringing her stuff and pampering her. And she liked that for a change of pace. So she kept not moving. But then, she saw them packing and wanted to come, so she snuck into her pack.

Dim laughed, "That's why it was so heavy. I thought I was just out of shape." She looked at the tinker, "You need to apologize when we get back." Glimmer's head sank. "I am glad that you came, though." She gave her a hug. "And that you're better."

"So, hon, now that that issue has been settled. What is going on?" Garrick turned to Dim.

The gnome tried to look busy unpacking, but really was just moving things around with no purpose. "Whatever do you mean?"

"Don't play that way, you know what I mean."

She looked at him, trying to keep a straight face, but couldn't. "I think I broke him."

"Who?" Garrick asked and was looking into the bag, expecting another tinker.

She slapped him on the arm. "Earch. I think he's broken now."

"What did you do?"

She just gave him a look. He went from confused to understanding, to shock.

"Yeah." She said.

"Oh." Garrick said. It all made sense to him now. Earch was always protective of Dim, but on this journey, he was being ridiculous. "Well, he'll probably settle down."

"You think so?"

Garrick was a good liar. In fact, he was a great liar. To be as successful of a rogue as he had been until now, as well as a good salesman, this was a necessary skill. To be able to tell a good yarn or to cover for not knowing what you were talking about and not let the other person know this was paramount.

Right here, with Dim, he just laughed.

Dim threw her head in her hands. She had to laugh herself.

"Maybe," Garrick said, "He has wanted this for a long, long time. He's going to be protective of it."

"I thought it would just be the same us, with some extra stuff." She said, sob-laughing into Garrick's shoulder now.

Garrick rubbed her hair to calm her. "I know, hon. You may need to let him know that, though."

"Me, why Do I have to?"

"You're the woman." He said, getting up as he noticed Earch coming back with an arm full of wood. "In my experience, in good relationships, the woman usually sets the tone." He went to help Earch set up the fire.

"It's cobolds. Looks like a lot of them, too."

Everybody except Bromm and Glimmer grunted. The latter mainly because she was of the right size to fight straight up with a cobold.

The former just looked at the others who were moaning or throwing sticks or doing some other discouraging looking thing. "What? They aren't tough."

"It's not that, they smell." Dim said. "Last time it took like a month to get the smell out of my hair."

"And messy. They're always blowing themselves up." Garrick said.

"Goblins blow themselves up."

"Yes, Bromm, but they do it on purpose. Cobolds are so random. One minute you're fighting one, then five just blow up for no reason. Splattering all over you." Zaela shook at the thought.

"I'll cover your hair with a spell." Earch told Dim, who just rolled her eyes at him. Garrick suppressed a laugh, but not well. The mage gave him a look.

"What is going on with you two, by the way? He's been following you around like a lost puppy." The elf said, then let out an understanding, "Oh." as Garrick gave her a look. She looked at Dim, then another "oh."

"Oh, what?" Bromm said.

"I'll fill you in later, big guy," Zaela told him.

Earch got up to say something, but Dim pulled him down, shaking her head. He looked at her, confused. She shook her head at him again and then sat next to her obediently. "I'll fill you in later, too." She told Zaela. "Should we move the camp?" She asked, trying desperately to change the subject.

The elf got the hint. "I don't think so. There are a lot of tracks, but they all seem old. Maybe keep a watch rotation."

"I will place some wards around, too," the mage said.

"Couldn't hurt."

"I have been placing them as we go anyway, just in case."

The elf looked at him. "Do you normally do that?"

"No, but since the warning from the..." Dim hit him.

"From the what?"

"You did not tell them?"

"No."

"You did not think that they should know?" Earch was quite upset.

The gnome looked at the others, "It was the Fear Gorta. He said 'I' could lose something." They were all looking at her now. "I didn't think it affected you."

Earch began casting. "Since we are with you, we all should know."

"Well, you knew. Why didn't you say something?" He grunted and wandered off. "You should have told us, but what's done is done." Bromm said. "Anyone want to back out now?" He looked at the others. They all, including Glimmer, shook their heads.

"I don't think the answer would have been different if we had known before, anyway." Garrick added, "Did it say anything else?"

"Just that it would fix everything with the farmers."

"Then we continue. Just be on your toes. That thing has been right before." Zaela looked at the gnome. Remembering the night of their encounter with the creature. How things would have been different if they had continued. But she was quite happy with Esus now, and apparently Dim was trying to make a go with Earch. So it may all work out in the end. Still, she had a small inkling to know what could have been if their timing was better.

They sat and ate. Earch sat between Zaela and Garrick to get some space from Dim, but that did not work well, since now he was across from her.

And it was odd.

Then it was a bit less odd. Then Glimmer got up and acted out her fight with the brute-man. I have already recanted this to you, but her version was much better. A lot more fighting was involved.

They all laughed and drank and sang a few songs to Garrick's lute, playing late into the night.

Chapter 18

Out of the Cobold Pan and Into the Fire Giants

The six of them, Dim, the gnome tinkerer, Garrick, the human rogue, Earch, the human mage, Zaela, the elf ranger, Bromm, the giant barbarian, and Glimmer, the tinker, well something, walked into the caverns in search of treasure to help pay off their debts and, of course, hopefully have a bit left over for the tavern. Dim could already taste a steak and cheese sandwich and one of those rum fizzies waiting for her.

Earch cast a lighting spell he had learned from the college that would illuminate their way for at least a few hours. At the very least, it would save on oil.

Zaela led the way, looking for signs of trouble and taking care of any minor problems that came about.

Bromm was behind her, just in case. The mage was close behind, staying by the gnome and shining his light so all could see. And Garrick took the rear, in case something tried to flank them.

Glimmer, for her part, rode in Dim's mended pack, watching for action.

There was little action to be seen. At least at first.

Then the cobolds came. And they came in waves. It wasn't exactly surprising, except that they seemed a bit more organized than how they had remembered the cobolds to be.

First, about twenty of the little creatures came running in. They, unfortunately for both the cobolds who died suddenly, and the party that was looking for a fight, blew themselves up.

As the group was trying to remove the bits and pieces of the first waves of cobolds from their clothes, the next wave came.

"This is gonna smell for months." Zaela said as she pulled a strip of cobold off of her shirt. "Might as well throw this away."

This wave was a bit more prepared and did not blow themselves up.

The first ten came through the cavern and met Zaela and Bromm. None did not get very far, five taken down by Zaela's swords and four by Bromm's maul in one swing. It took the four and slammed them hard against the wall, causing a crumbling in the roof and a not very encouraging sound. Zaela turned to Bromm and motioned to be careful.

The last one smartly ran from the first rank and straight at Dim. She raised her knives to strike him but hit an invisible barrier, as did the cobold. It slammed itself at full speed and slumped over. Then exploded all over the invisible shield.

Dim looked to Earch and put her hands up as if to say 'what the hells?' Earch saw the next wave coming and decided to try to avoid this conversation altogether, moving up to where Bromm stood. Ten dart-like missiles flew from his fingers, picking off the next ten cobolds. They fell lifeless in front of them.

Zaela moved back towards the gnome. "What happened there?" She asked her.

"He put a damned shield on me."

"Why? It's a cobold. You could probably kill it by accident."

"Apparently, I'm not allowed to fight anymore."

"Your boyfriend needs boundaries." Zaela said as she sliced a cobold that made it through.

"I hate that word," Dim said, sitting down. There wasn't much else to do. Glimmer ran straight into another cobold and took it out, jumping up and looking for more. Dim pointed both hands at the tinker in disappointment.

"Well, you could have had a girlfriend." the elf winked at her while taking another cobold down.

She stuck her tongue out at her. "I thought that you were happy with Esus."

"I am, I am," she said, although the double 'I am' made Dim think the opposite. "It's just, well, interesting to think what we would have been like." She sliced at another cobold, but missed it. It ran straight into Dim's shield and staggered back. Glimmer jumped on it and began pounding her fists into it.

"The timing..." Dim started.

"... was off. I know." Zaela finished. "Just a fun 'what if?' I guess?" More were coming now, and Zaela had to pay a little attention to the battle.

Dim sat in her shield while cobolds bounced off of her. Thinking a little more about the 'what if?' The cobold attack halted.

Another rumble came, and they all looked at Bromm. Bromm looked back and shrugged. A few hundred cobolds stacked the cavern floor. It wasn't him. And it wasn't an explosion.

The rumble came again.

Louder.

Then they saw it. It was like an avalanche of cobolds, mainly running except the first few, which flew past them as if thrown from a catapult. Bromm knocked one out of the air and it exploded upon the others. Well, except for Dim, who grimaced as it splattered in front of her on the shield. Now she not only couldn't fight, but couldn't see either.

Zaela, Earch and Bromm tried to keep up with the onslaught, Earch firing spells to take out the invading force, Bromm with his maul and Zaela her swords. But, the cobolds were not attacking.

They weren't even defending themselves.

They were just running. And running in terror.

Although the front line took out many, and Garrick took a few. Even Glimmer was pounding upon one. They kept running, trying to escape, something.

The party eventually stopped fighting the cobolds, at least those that they could avoid. Dim looked up. This cavern was huge, and now that she looked at it in closer, it was relatively freshly made. This was not a cobold lair. At least not anymore. Maybe it once was.

"Run!" Zaela said as she passed them.

They turned and ran for the entrance, following the cobolds. A boulder was moving to cover the entrance. Some cobolds escaped. Some were squished by the stone. The next wave trapped and trampled many more.

Something was coming. Something big.

The rumbling grew closer, louder. The shield that had protected and inhibited Dim began to flicker and wane in power. Glimmer climbed back into her pack.

The party was almost with the cobolds now, but they just cowered in fear, posing no threat. The party turned and prepared. Whatever was coming was coming fast. Bromm held his maul, Zaela her swords, Earch his staff and Dim her knives. The gnome tossed a knife to

Glimmer, who was not expecting it. It clanged off her and fell to the ground with a twang. She held her hands up to her creator in a similar 'what the Hells was that?' gesture that Dim had just given to Earch, then picked it up.

The cobolds were behind them. Their fear made them continue to trample each other as the sounds became louder and closer. The party was ready for whatever was to come. At least they thought they were.

But then it came. A hideous giant, twice as large at least as Bromm, smacked their giant aside as if he were a toy. He hit the wall of the cavern without the time to react. Dim watched as her friend hit the wall and went limp, falling to the ground.

Zaela launched herself into the giant's eyes and stabbed them, blinding it.

Garrick came and stabbed the giant in a place that will not be mentioned, but the giant fell and fell hard. Dim went straight for Bromm to check on him. He would need aid later, but could fight on. He struck the giant with his maul, crushing its head with a thunderous crack!

The party sat, out of breath. Earch mainly came equipped with protection spells for Dim, and he cast them all. They could hear the rumble coming, louder than before.

More were coming, and just the one had almost killed Bromm.

Dim took Glimmer to her breast and held her. She did not want to lose the tinker again, so soon after the last time. Earch drew close to them, as did Garrick. Bromm and Zaela, ever the heroes, took the lead. The cobolds cowered.

"It's a trap!" Zaela said.

Dim's first thoughts was that Esus and Mallory had done this. They would die here and they were the responsible.

But the map came not from Mallory. It came from...

Next to her, a break in reality appeared. A round portal pulling her towards it. She called for the others as she went into it, but they could not hear her.

They apparently could not see it either.

Only she and Glimmer were pulled inside. At the last moment, she saw Earch look at her and call out. He faded away from a solid, to transparent, to a ghostly shape, to just gone. She reached to him as he reached to her. She had felt his touch for a moment, but that, too, faded away.

She was somewhere else. She and Glimmer were, for the moment, out of danger. But. where they were, they did not know.

Chapter 19

The Melted Cheese Between the Worlds

The portal opened to the swamp where she had met the gnome wizard before, although this time, no dragon stood in front of her. The swamp did, however.

"Greetings!" the wizard said. "I trust that you have destroyed my hut by now!"

"Hut?" Dim asked. She truly could not remember what the other gnome was talking about.

"The hut." the wizard took her arm and pulled her deeper into his sanctuary. "The hut. I gave you the box to find the hut and destroy it."

"The box?" Moving from one world to the next had obviously disoriented Dim. The fear of a giant on one and of a dragon on the next did not help. "I know of no hut."

"I gave you the box."

"Yes."

"It led you to the hut."

"No."

"It did not?"

"No."

"What did it do then?"

"Powered my farm equipment."

"Powered your farm equipment?"

"Yes."

"Really?"

"Yes."

They had entered a deeper chamber, one filled with what appeared to be many ancient artifacts. Dim found a seat and sat. It was an emotional day so far.

"You used the artifact that I gave you to power farm equipment?"

"Yes."

"Did you not think that it was more powerful than that?"

Dim sat up. She was in no mood for questioning her decisions. "You gave no instructions."

"You were late."

"Late?"

"Yes, yes. You were supposed to be in the bog at least five minutes earlier."

Dim looked at Glimmer. Glimmer looked at Dim. Both had a look of extreme confusion with a tinge of anger. Both looked back at the wizard.

"Well, at least that was the plan." He said, not at all liking the looks on the women's faces. "You try to figure out time in twenty or so different worlds all at once and then see how difficult it is."

"I have enough trouble with one."

The wizard pointed at her knowingly and nodded. "See, see. Yes, one is hard enough. That damned hut..." He trailed off with some more choice words about the hut.

"So, about the hut," Dim said.

"You found it!" Gallila said.

"No. No, I did not. What exactly is it? I mean, like a house type hut?"

"Well, yes. Maybe. I'm not entirely sure really in this world." He scampered to look at some scrolls and a weird device.

"So how am I supposed to find it if you don't even know what I'm looking for?"

"The box." He said absently, but with a tone that made Dim feel dumb that she did not know that.

"The box."

"Yes. It's like a map, or a compass, sort of, to the hut."

"And there are twenty huts?"

The wizard looked up at her. "Why would there be twenty?"

"You said..."

"No, one hut." Dim could tell he was getting frustrated at this point. She just was not sure if it was at her or himself.

He seemed to be making some calculations; Dim looked around, not wanting to bother him. Finally, he laughed, "Ah, it was your fault all along!"

"What was?"

"Why you were late."

"Late? To the meeting I did not know about?"

"Yes! You stayed at the tavern too long! I knew it wasn't me."

"What?"

"The tavern. You were supposed to hear about the quest, then leave. But you stayed longer. Or went back in. It was your fault. Those sandwiches are wonderful, by the way."

It took her a moment, but she realized what was going on. "You're the Fear Gorta."

"Of course."

"So you basically tricked me into going to get your stupid box?" Dim said, quite angry now, "And stole my sandwiches!"

The wizard looked at her, realizing that he may be in danger. 'Was it because of the sandwich?' he wondered. "Technically, you gave it to me."

"Thinking you were a Fear Gorta!" she yelled. Visibly upset now.

The wizard understood it was a great sandwich. 'Amazing what they can do with cattle these days,' he had thought when he ate it the first time. "It was quite yummy." He told her. "I was quite disappointed at first that it was not the meat pie. But, once I tasted it..." He paused and relived the moment. "At least it was not that moldy cheese again."

"It was all I had."

"You had ham!"

She grunted. This was going nowhere and her friends may be in trouble. She really just wanted to get back and away from whatever the Hells this was.

Sensing her frustration, the wizard moved on. "If you just give me the box, I can show you how it works. Then you can defeat the hut. I can go on my way, and all will be well."

Dim looked at the man. "I, um, don't have it." She said.

"Ah, that's a problem, now isn't it?" the gnome wizard said. "Where is it now?"

"I don't know, possibly with Mallory?" Dim said.

"Possibly, possibly." the wizard walked around the room. "Anyone else that may have it?"

Dim went to answer, but it did not seem like the wizard was talking to her. Glimmer sat down and seemed to mimic sleeping. Dim looked at her, was about to chastise her for disrespect, but then thought better of it. She was right. This was going to be a long day.

"I normally, in most worlds, would think the slender one would steal it, but I don't know. She seems to be stricken with your friend in this world. But, if the brute has it..." He tailed off.

"What if the brute has it?"

The wizard paced faster. He started to speak, but then stopped for a second. Dim rolled her index and middle finger at him, telling him to speed it up. "It would be disastrous for your village, for one." He paused and then watched as Dim's fingers kept twirling. "And probably your world." He said in a much lower volume.

"My what?" Dim asked.

The wizard turned away, but still answered louder, "Your world."

Dim's face went green. Glimmer even seemed to move a little, but she was quite content laying where she was. She turned so that she could see the action a little better. If she knew what popcorn was, and also could eat it, she would want some right now.

"So," Dim started. Glimmer knew that if Dim started with the word 'so' that it was not good for who she was talking to. She was about to tell things the way they should be told. There may be no agreeable solution, but someone definitely messed up, usually Little Al, but somebody. And now the gnome was going to let that somebody know that they, indeed, had messed up. "So," she repeated. This was going to be a major one. "This box that you gave me is going to be, and I quote 'disastrous' for my home and world! All to find some stupid hut that I wouldn't know what to do with if I found it, anyway. Which, as far as I know, has nothing to do with me at all. What the Hells are you going to do about this!" Although her volume rose quite high, it was a bit of a letdown for Glimmer. She was expecting more. Really, like a two out of ten on her scorecard.

The wizard sat down, tired of all the pacing, it seemed. "Well, like I told you, you used the box wrong. And you were late."

"So," there it was again, "you're telling me that because I was late to something that I did not even know about. This is all my fault!"

"Exactly!" He touched his nose. Apparently, that meant something.

Dim picked up the nearest thing and threw it towards the wizard. Not to hit him, exactly, but just to get some aggression out. Whatever it was smashed to pieces a few feet from him.

"Also, that dragon wouldn't have tried to attack us, now would it have?" The wizard pointed out matter-of-factually. "I saved you from it, you know?" he waited for the thank you. He didn't wait long. The thank you also didn't come.

"You dragged me there!" She threw something else. It did not break, but clunked into the wall and fell, dented. This one was closer. Glimmer thought that the wizard should probably stop soon, as Dim really had impeccable aim and could have hit him twice already. "And how did leaving the tavern later even make a difference?"

"Everything affects everything else," He said, quite to the point.

"How do you propose" she paused when she said it. "We" then paused again, "get it back, then?" Then lifted another artifact.

"Don't throw that one." The wizard-gnome said. And when Dim gave him a look, he added, "That might destroy reality a bit." He scrunched his fingers together, showing how much reality might be destroyed. She put it down carefully, picking up another, pointed it at him. He nodded, and she threw it closer than the last one. "I can't help you." the wizard stated and turned back to his maps.

Dim picked up the 'reality-destroying' object again and set it up shot-put style, aiming at the wizard. "And why is that? Do. Not. Say. Anything. About. A. Stupid. HUT!"

The wizard paused. Looked at her and couldn't think of anything else. "The hut may find me."

Dim screamed and threw the object at the wizard gnome. He dodged it, barely, and then sank into the fetal position. Dim dove for cover, and on seeing that Glimmer did not move, pulled the tinker to her and covered her as well.

After what seemed like a few minutes and a whole lot of nothing happening, the wizard laughed. Then he coughed and possibly choked. Dim and Glimmer were concerned for a moment, but the man came too after a bit.

"I'm sorry, that was the wrong orb." He began his laughing fit again. After stopping, he shook his head, "I should have gone with another boy Dim."

"A what?"

"Boy Dim."

"There are boy Dims?"

"Yes. Of course. One cat Dim and a tinker Dim I met once too. They are way too temperamental to deal with, though." Glimmer looked up at him in a scowl. "No offense."

Glimmer waved him off. "Why a boy?"

"They listen to wizards and just do what they're told. Less messy. Boy Dims are great."

"Why Dims?"

"I needed a gnome."

"But, why Dims?" She repeated.

"Have you met any gnomes? No, of course not, you're a Dim." He decided that now might be a good time to sit. "Gnomes, in general, don't do much. I mean, they tend to work hard, but they just don't go any-where. They sit in their gardens or mine the caves. They don't really venture out."

"And?"

"Well, you do. Not just here, but every world."

"Every..."

He interrupted, "Well, every world that I have been to."

"How many are there?"

"Damned if I know. I've been to twenty-two so far."

"But how?"

"Worlds are, well, like your sandwich."

"How are worlds like my sandwich?"

"I'm getting there. Do you happen to have one?" The wizard looked at her with intense interest.

"No."

The interest waned, "So, like your yummy sandwich, the worlds are in these layers. You have the meat layers, the onion parts, the pepper parts, even the salt parts..."

"The salt parts?"

"Yes, tinier worlds. I mean, if you're in them, they seem just as big as the others, but they are tiny in comparison. And delicious." He stopped and thought of the sandwich again. "You are quite sure that you don't have one?"

"Salt."

"No, a sandwich."

"Where would I be carrying a sandwich?"

"Maybe in your bag..." He tilted his head twice, seeming to indicate back in her world.

"No." Dim was having a tough time with this conversation, but his sandwich talk reminded her of her world and the battle. She stood and dusted herself off. She got Glimmer to her feet as well and addressed the wizard. "Can you at least do some sort of whooshy thing and get us back to my world? My friends were in a bit of a mess."

He waved her off, "Oh don't worry about them, at least not yet." He tailed off, then tried to continue, "The cheese..."

Dim interrupted this time, "Yet?"

"Oh yeah, two of them are in grave danger soon." He licked his lips, "The melted..."

"Two?" Dim was pacing now. "Who?"

"Two of the males. The elf, I think, will be okay."

"I need to get back."

"There's little you can do. Well, about one. You actually get to choose, kind of, for the other."

"How do I save one?"

"I don't know. Something that you say. Now where was I?"

"Getting me back."

"No, that's not it." He massaged his beard in a thinking way. "You'll be back almost simultaneously as when you left, anyway. Oh yeah! Cheese!"

"What?"

"The cheese is the most important part."

"I have no idea what's going on."

"The cheese touches everything, the bread, the meat, the onions and peppers, the salt. Everything."

"So?"

"You need to get into the cheese to travel the worlds. It touches them all."

"Oh."

"Plus, it's gooey."

"The cheese?"

"Yes, and the places between worlds. Usually gooey." He looked around the cave. It was a bit gooey.

Dim shook her head. At this point, she did not know what was going on, except that the wizard might be mad. She decided to cut to the chase. "What, exactly, do you want me to do?" She figured this may be the only way to get back to save Earch. Or Garrick. Or Bromm.

"I thought that I told you." The wizard said.

Dim pinched the top of her nose. "No. You were talking about sandwiches."

"Ah, yes." He seemed to go back into his mind again. "Do you have one?"

"No!" Dim yelled.

This startled the wizard and made him think that she was going to throw things again. Best to get rid of her now. He started conjuring the portal. "Find the box, follow it to the hut, destroy the hut."

"Then you'll leave me alone?"

"Of course!" She heard him say as she took Glimmer and stepped into the portal. As she slipped back into her real world, she heard the gnome's voice fading away at the same time she saw Earch's hand fading back into sight. She grabbed the hand as she heard the voice say, "Probably."

Chapter 20

The Loss

"We can't take them. We have to retreat."

"There is no way out. It's blocked."

"We have to try. Garrick, see if there are any weak spots in the barricade."

"Something may just be behind it, waiting to pick us off."

"Well, something's up here about to pick us off!"

Earch cast something. "This better not be some protection spell just for me." Dim yelled at him.

"Shh. I need to concentrate," the wizard said. He was listening. "Garrick, to the left, there's something."

"You need to stop babying me."

"I am not, I am listening."

"To what?"

"Garrick, to the left, there's something."

"God, these things smell so bad," the rogue yelled, slicing through the cobolds to get to the left. "It's small."

"Is it open?"

"It can be. All back!"

The rumbling grew louder; the ground shook. Dim estimated that it was at least five of the giants coming. The cobolds had found the opening and were pulling at it, squeezing their way through. The party would have to wait them out, but they would do the work of opening it.

"It's too small."

"You'll fit, Little Thief." Bromm put his hand on her shoulder.

"But..." She looked up at her friend. She saw in his eyes that his mind was made up and he was not coming with them. There was no time.

Bromm's hand touched the stag that he made her that lay near her heart.

"I am with you, always."

"No." the gnome said.

"We have no choice." He turned to Zaela, "I will hold them off as long as I can, but they will try to follow you."

The rumbling and shaking grew stronger. The elf hugged the giant, tears in her eyes. "I will miss you, friend."

They heard the fire giants talking as a cobold flew past their heads. "You must go," Bromm said as they turned to see Dim and Glimmer trying to pull the wall apart.

"You must go, Dim." This startled the gnome out of a daze. Bromm had only called her Dim on a very few occasions, most of them not good. She turned to him, her face a mess with tears and blubbery. She could not have said anything, even if words had come to her. "It is not your fault."

"It is."

"It's all of ours. We all made bad choices to get here. We all misjudged."

"What do you mean?"

"I am uncertain, but someone betrayed us." He picked her up and placed her in the hole in the wall. "I will see you again. I feel it. Maybe in another world. Now go."

Glimmer looked at him with her head down. "You too, little one. There is no good you can do here." He patted her brass head. The first of the fire giant turned into the hall. "Go." Bromm yelled.

Glimmer watched as her giant friend turned and ran towards the giant and struck its head with his maul.

'He has a chance.' the brass girl beeped as she turned to join the others.

The party ran through what was left of a corridor, following the cobolds, who, in their panic, were posing no threat to them. Each of them trying to come to terms with the fact that they had just lost one of their own.

Dim held the stag tight, trying to give her friend some extra power, or luck, or anything really.

They reach a point where the cobolds were climbing through again. Daylight beamed from the other side.

"Oh god!" Esus yelled from the other side. "What is that smell?"

"Esus!" Zaela yelled and ran through the small creatures to the hole.

"Zaela! Thank the gods you're alright. You've been betrayed."

"Yes, we figured. Who?"

"I'm not sure who's the brains are, but we tracked down my former partner."

"You're sure it's not Mallory?" Dim asked between sobs as she was pulled after Zaela from the cave.

"Yes, but the brute, as you call him, and some others defected to, well, another boss. They are somewhere near, I think. We have to go."

"Who do they work for? Why should we trust you?"

Esus looked at the gnome and saw the hurt on her face. "As for who, I think that you would know better than I. As for trust, I can't answer that. But I risked my life to be here." She hugged Zaela tight. Worry dripped from her face as Garrick and Earch exited the hole.

"No big guy?"

Everyone lowered their heads. After a moment, Garrick got them moving back towards the village.

Esus was right, the Brute and his people were waiting for any survivors outside the cavern. They had only a moment before the arrows and bolts came. Not to mention the pounding on the rock wall. Bromm did not hold the giants back long. (To be fair, he killed two of them and wounded another. Two more than anyone, even he, would have thought.)

There was no time to grieve, though, only to run.

Luckily for them, the Brute had expected that if they made it out, they would have to use the original entrance, not where they had dug themselves from. After some cobolds made their way through, though, they had tried to reconfigure, but it spread them thin, covering two exits.

The band ran for the woods and then towards the village. Bor looked up as they ran past him and followed them after a day or two. No one bothered him at all.

"Where are we heading?" Garrick asked, "They'll probably have all our houses under watch."

"Bromm's?" Earch said.

"Anyone at the village won't know he's..." Zaela could not finish the sentence.

"Mrs. Appleby's, then?" Garrick asked.

"I don't think that's a good idea." Dim said and lowered her head.

Earch looked at her. "Why?"

"If Esus is right, and Mallory isn't behind this..."

"It's not Mallory. I swear."

"Right, then, if she isn't. Who else in the village has the resources to pay these people?"

"But why?" Earch asked.

The gnome just shook her head. Everyone sat quietly for a bit, trying to think of a place that they could go where they could rest and figure things out.

Finally Dim spoke up, "My parent's house." She said coldly and stood. She grabbed her pack and began walking. Earch went to say something, but Zaela stopped him. "I'll scout it out."

"I'm coming, too." Esus said and followed.

Garrick looked at Earch, and then Dim's face and decided he did not want to hear what was about to be said if this conversation started, "I'll go, um, cover our tracks. You good, hon?"

"No." Dim said. "But go. We don't want anyone following us, if we can help it."

The rogue saluted her and started off. Glimmer beeped at him and he swept her up. "Looks like the little lady wants to come."

Dim waved her hand at him absentmindedly and he was off.

"Are you going to be alright going back there?" The mage asked.

Dim thought for a moment. "I'll have to be." Then she turned to him, "What the Hells was that?"

"What?"

"Don't 'what?' me. You trapped me in a shield and put wards all around." She was in his face now. "For the good they did."

"Yeah." Earch said. He slunked to the ground. She wanted to yell at him. Wanted to blame him for everything, but she knew it wasn't true. She wanted to blame anyone but herself, but she also saw the defeat in his face. "I messed up. I panicked when I saw the cobolds coming."

"I could have helped."

"I know. It's just..." He shrugged. "I do not know."

She went to him and sat next to him. She put his hand in hers. "Trust me."

"I do."

"You can not do that again."

He looked into her eyes. "I can not promise you that, but I will try."

Dim smiled at him and kissed him. "That's all I ask."

"It's clear." Zaela said as she came through the clearing. I checked everywhere. No sign of anyone for months.

They walked to the house once Garrick returned. Dim laid her hand over the door. The door she had gone through so many times as a child and teen. The door that her father had made when he had built the house.

She turned the knob and pushed in. The gnome was a child again for a moment, but it subsided. She walked into her parents' house for the first time in months.

For only the second time since her mother died.

Chapter 21

We All Smell a Little

The group mourned a little for the loss of Bromm, but for the most part, that was going to have to wait. They had lost group members before, of course, but not one of the main five. They had lost a few rookies, but not anyone for a while.

Bromm's loss was going to sting. They all had liked him. He had touched them all in one way or another. And he died to save them. You just can't forget that.

Even if they had trouble admitting it to themselves or each other, they all had become friends.

Dim told the other's of what the gnome wizard had told her. I would get into it now, but you were there with me, so that would be redundant. So I'll just say that they were quite skeptical.

The box, however, they could not dismiss. They had all seen it. And they all knew what it could do.

Esus also attested to the fact that if the box was now in the hands of the brute, and if it was nearly as powerful as the wizard had said, everyone was in danger. The man loved to have, and to flaunt, power.

Dim thought that it may be worse. She had known Mrs. Appleby for all her life. She had always been a role model, the nicest of nice. If she had set this all up to gain the box, it must have corrupted her. Or something worse. Something bigger than the box. If anyone had taken control of the hut, that could spell doom for more than the village or even the world.

She shuddered to think about that.

"... through the tunnels to Mallory." Esus was talking when Dim started paying attention again. Dim tilted her head a little, trying to figure out what she was talking about.

"Under the city." Earch told her, like that, cleared anything up. The gnome's eyebrows raised an inch.

Zaela huffed, but took control. "Dim, there are tunnels under the city."

"I know. Me and Earch used to play in them. Until they started collapsing."

"A little after that as well," the mage reminded her.

"A little, yes. What about them?"

Esus was clearly upset, but Dim figured it out. "You want ME to go through the tunnels?"

Esus nodded.

"How do we know they are still there?"

"They're there. I've been in them. It's how we traveled the city under cover." Esus told her.

"Why don't you go," the gnome said. Clearly, they had already talked about this while Dim wasn't paying attention. Everyone, even Glimmer, threw up their hands at this point.

"Collapsed." Dim said.

Everyone nodded.

"Mallory had wanted me to come out here and see if we could find anything to, well, help with the Dim problem."

"The Dim problem. You had a name for me." Dim was actually excited about this.

"Yes, as I am sure you did for us. Probably a bit more wordy, though."

"The Mallory problem." Garrick said.

Esus laughed, "Really?"

Zaela nodded. "So, Esus thinks you might be able to get through."

"Hells, how long was I daydreaming?"

"Quite a while, hon."

"Does it still stink down there?"

Garrick gave her a look. "Any more than you already do?" Everyone laughed at this.

"You don't smell so fresh yourself." It was good to laugh. It had been a horrible day so far and now she had to find her way to Mallory's house climbing through tunnels that she had not been in since she was a child.

"Where's all your protecting me now, mage?" Dim eyed Earch.

"You told me not to."

"But, for this? If you know of the tunnels, doesn't the brute?"

"He does," Esus said. "Avoid his men."

"It could be a trap." She said, mainly to herself. Esus narrowed her eyes at her. Dim pulled her attention to Earch. "You're okay with this?"

"I learned my lesson. It is your decision." He came close and hugged her. "I'll back you up. Either way."

"I guess I'm going then. Are you in, Glim?" The tinker sat in the corner, slumped down and barely moving. She looked at the gnome and twirled her two fingers in the Dim fashion. "No way I can get that extra special keep me out of danger Earch back now?"

The mage smiled, but shook his head. "Not a chance." He said and kissed her deeply.

Dim looked to the sun. It seemed to have not moved since they went into the cavern.

The Plan was quite simple. Glimmer and Dim would try to get to Mallory through the tunnels while Zaela and Esus attempted to get close to Mrs. Appleby's and gather information. Garrick and Earch would devise a plan, try to get supplies, and prepare new spells.

Dim's part was probably the most dangerous, but besides Glimmer, she was the only one of them that could do it, according to Esus.

Whom she still did not fully trust.

It was not long before she believed her in this aspect, however. They quickly got to a passage that was almost completely caved in. Glimmer made it through with little trouble, but when the gnome tried to get through, she caught her pants half way.

She sat there for a moment, trying to untangle herself.

"This is all I need," she looked at Glimmer, who just looked impatient. "I'll either die here or make it to Mallory's with no pants."

Glimmer raised her hands and then pointed them towards the way they need to go.

"Alright, alright." Dim said and tried to continue wiggling her way through. "I don't know what's up with you."

Glimmer whirred in frustration to the gnome and wandered off.

"Hells! Damn those sandwiches." Dim yelled as she heard a rip and her hips loosened on the cave in debris. She pulled herself free and tried to secure her pants to stay up.

Glimmer came back at that point, beeping and whirring about how she, too, was friends with the giant. And that she, too, was sad. And that she, too, was concerned about the box and was quite, at this moment, miserable. But then she saw the mess that was Dim. She just started laughing at her.

Between her normally messy hair also being caked with mud and cobold guts, along with the rest of her body, and her standing there holding her pants up with one hand and holding her broken belt missing one of her daggers in the other, as with also somehow loosing a shoe, the tinker could not help herself. This sight had been the only thing to give her any joy at all since the Bromm incident.

She fell over, laughing harder than she ever had.

Dim just sat and put her face in her hands and cried.

It was a long, hard, ugly cry. Glimmer felt for her and came over to give her a hug, but when the gnome looked up, the mud and guts had washed in streaks from her eyes.

Glimmer tried not to, but chuckled anyway.

Dim turned and reached back to where she came to grab her bag. She couldn't quite reach so stretched further, losing hold of her pants. Glimmer lost it at that point and could not control herself.

Dim looked at the tinker and her mind tore itself between crying and having a fit, or laughing and having a fit. She chose the latter and held the brass girl to her, laughing at themselves and their predicament. "We really are in it now, aren't we?" she said, more to herself.

After their fits subsided, Dim looked through her travel pack, looking for anything that may help keep her pants on, at least for a few hours. She was pulling out gears and a lever and more gears along with scrap metal and tools.

"Dammit, it has to still be here." She said, now frantically rummaging through what was left. Finally, her hand touched the case. It felt like gold. Finding what she thought was not still there, and she had not used in forever.

The sewing kit!

So there she sat, in a tunnel that she almost got herself stuck in for eternity, that she was quite sure was some sort of sewer by the smell. "How did I not remember this smell before?" she asked at one point. Pantsless, trying to sew, which she was never good at, hungry and cold.

She figured that boys had probably bathed and found food by now. They most likely were sitting around eating and drinking to Bromm at this point. "Hells!" she said for about the fifth time as she poked herself again, this time drawing blood.

She went back into her bag for alcohol. Mainly for the tiny prick on her finger, but also for a taste. It wasn't much, but it helped.

Glimmer looked as the gnome put her pants back on and stood up. "I know. They looked horrible." Glimmer waved her hand around, indicating that everything about her looked horrible.

"You're not so hot yourself right now Glim." The gnome said. "Can you look for my other dagger while I put this stuff away? I want to end this. Then have some wine and a bath." Glimmer nodded and went back into the hole. Coming out a moment later, holding the lost dagger.

Chapter 22

I'm On a Boat!

T he two women made their way down the tunnel, trying to figure out about where they were and which way to turn every time a choice was to be made. Dim's pants, mostly, stayed up with the help of a tug and adjustment now and again.

It was not a professional job, or even a good one, but it sufficed.

They ran into a few tight fitting areas, but nothing like the first one where she had gotten stuck.

At about the halfway point by Dim's calculations (Glimmer had other ideas, but no real argument came from it, mainly because Dim just shrugged her shoulders when Glimmer tried to make it one) They heard voices.

They also came to a fork in the tunnel, which led to an argument.

"It's right." Dim said.

Glimmer twirled her finger by her head, pointed at Dim and then pointed left.

"I am not mixed up, it's right."

The brass girl beeped and whirred at her in protest. She was quite adamant that the correct path would be to the left. Hands were flying and beeps were beeping.

"I trust you, I do. But I am sure it's right."

At that moment, they heard a voice. "What's that?" It said.

Another voice answered, "Don't know, go check it out."

"Why don't you?"

"I'm in charge."

"In charge of what? We're in a smelly hole."

"Whatever it was, it probably left now, listening to you."

"Shut up." And the talking stopped. Footsteps came their way. Not fast at all. More like the sound that someone who absolutely did not want to do a certain job but had to anyway, so they were giving it the minimal amount of effort possible would make.

Glimmer seemed gung-ho to take on the guards, which Dim was pretty sure that they could. By the time the first one knew they were there, they'd be down to one.

But then, the other one may run and alert others. That would not be ideal.

Besides, she had seen too much death lately. If she could get through just this day without another person dying, she would be, maybe happy is not the correct word, but it would be better at the least. "You said left.

Let's go left." She told Glimmer, pulled up her pants without thinking, and started walking as quietly as she could.

Glimmer huffed, but followed. At least she won one argument.

Dim kept a listen as the conversation between the two men kept going. "There's nothing here."

"I didn't think there would be."

"Why the Hells did you send me then?"

"Partly to see if you'd go."

There was a pause. "Fair enough. I didn't sign up to sit in a sewer all day."

"Me neither."

And so on. Surprisingly, she could hear them for quite some time. She had to remember to keep the noise to a minimum.

"How much longer?" She whispered to Glimmer.

Glimmer shrugged her shoulders in a 'Hells if I know' sort of way.

"I thought I was following you," the gnome said and pushed to the front. "Gods, we'll be stuck in here forever."

Glimmer excitedly pointed at something, ironically a glimmer in the tunnel's ceiling. It was small and faint, but there.

"It must be a grate." Dim said, as they got closer. I bit of water trickled through and as they approach, the murmur of the village center became audible. "I think we're right near the tavern."

Glimmer pounded her chest in triumph.

"Don't be so proud of yourself yet. We haven't quite made it."

The brass girl pounded her chest again in defiance.

"We're still a-ways away, but at least we know where we are."

Glimmer whirred and put her arms up.

"Yes, yes. You always knew. I'm sure."

"You hear that?" A voice came from above them. Dim put her finger to her lips, but Glimmer was in a panic.

The gnome grabbed her and pulled her away from the grate, as someone was trying to clear it. "What is it?" She whispered. The tinker was shaking like Dim had never felt. She held her close to her.

"It's them."

"How do you know?" Another said.

"I know. We need to get to the tunnels."

It was a familiar voice. Dim knew why Glimmer panicked. The brute had found them. "Let's go!" Dim yelled to the tinker.

Glimmer held up her arms to ask, 'where?'

Dim didn't know. She just knew that here would not work. Nor going back the way they had come. Taking on two lowly henchmen with surprise was one thing. Taking on a brute without it was completely another.

So they ran.

Glimmer was in a complete state of panic. All the things that the brute had done to her came back and

her mind went numb. Dim actually wasn't too far behind in the panic department, either. They ran as fast
as they could, choosing paths willy-nilly as they
reached each turn in the tunnels.

No matter how fast they ran, a bit of light followed
them. As did the brute and his men's voices.

They couldn't make out what they were saying, although Dim could not tell if that was because of the
echo or their frantic states of mind. Either way, it did
not matter. They knew that he was behind them. And
they knew that if he caught them, he would kill them.
Probably in the most horrible way he could think of.

Dim's mind left her for a moment, thinking of what
Molly and Little Al would do when they didn't come
back. If they were okay, that was. She had not thought
of that before. The brute or his men may have already
taken them out. She hoped they ran at the first sign of
trouble. And Earch too. Dim didn't want to hold herself
up too high on a pedestal, but what the Hells would he
do without her? Hopefully, he'd move on, but she did
not know.

Garrick and Zaela would be okay. But losing her,
Glimmer, and Bromm in a day's time. Dim didn't wish
that on anyone.

She thought about all this as she ran. If you asked
her which way she had turned at any of the forks, she
would not have even known that there was a turn. She
wouldn't even have remembered that she had pulled

her pants up about forty-seven times in this short period.

She shook her head. This train of thought would do no good. They had to survive.

That was the thought in her head when the ground seemed to disappear. One foot went out in front of her as the other did not.

She ended up sliding down a forty-five degree slope in the splits, a brass girl in front of her, and an unknown destination coming up. Dim figured that it would be a wall or a hole. This was the end.

It was a wall. It was not quite the end, at least not yet, but her ankle that was in front of her slammed hard into stone. She yelled out and tried to cover her mouth, but some sound had already escaped. Her ankle throbbed, but the adrenaline was pushing most of the pain away after the initial hit.

"Here kitty kitty." The brute said from where she had started her slide. "I'm coming to get ya."

Glimmer and Dim had three choices. Left, right or face the brute. Glimmer certainly was in no mental shape to face him and Dim's ankle, although she could walk for now, wouldn't hold up in battle.

They chose left.

The two ran, Dim with a limp, and came to a locked gate that opened up to the hillside. The gnome rattled the metal and tried to push it open. It wiggled, but would not budge. Dim pulled her bag and searched through it, desperate to find her old lock picks.

"I'm coming to git ya," she heard the brute say, and she heard his controlled slide down the shaft. "Don't you worry now."

She found the picks and pulled it out, desperately reaching for the lock. The first pick broke with her shaking hand almost immediately. She pulled another and wiggled into the lock.

"Almost there." He said. The footsteps were closer and closer. He was going slowly, taunting them. He must have known that they were trapped.

She twisted the metal pick. Felt it click. Felt the lock open.

Glimmer beeped a horrid beep.

"I thought I killed you already." The brute said, looking straight at the tinker.

The door swung open and Glimmer dove off the side of the hill.

Dim grabbed her bag and followed, sliding down the muddy path, through the muck that exited the drains of the village.

"There's nowhere to hide!" the brute yelled at them as they lay at the bottom of the hill in a river of sludge.

Dim was tired. She was more tired than she ever remembered being. Now she lay in a river that carried the waste of her city out to the sea, at least at some point. She was actually surprised by how clean it was, considering. At least compared to her and Glimmer.

Dim looked to the sun, "Something is wrong."

Glimmer just looked at the gnome with a face that explained that everything was wrong.

"Yes, I know. But the sun hasn't moved." She pointed up at it.

The brass girl whirred her understanding, but at the same time said that it was not their most pressing concern at this exact moment.

"True." Dim heard the Brute's men coming towards them, but they were a ways off still. "I think we're done for now, Glim." Dim said and dropped her head into the mucky bank. "I don't think there's anywhere we can go."

Glimmer beeped a little. She was wearing down. "Need a wind?" Glimmer put her hands up slowly, which Dim took as to say 'does it matter?' "You could probably get away," the gnome said, as she turned the brass girl's key. "I think they'd leave you alone if they got me."

Glimmer looked irked by this. Why wouldn't they want to get her too, huh? She could be dangerous to whatever they were doing, couldn't she? What were they doing anyway and why were they targeting a no name gnome and a tinker girl? It seemed strange to her.

"I wonder if they'll kill me right away or take me prisoner?" Dim said.

Glimmer hopped up and looked around. She noticed a small boat stuck in the muck. Pointing and hollering, she hopped up and down, tapping Dim as she did.

"I saw it, doesn't look like it will float." Though she lifted herself up on her elbows to look at it though.

Glimmer went into a series of pantomimes, during which she chastised the gnome for being lazy and giving up while also telling her how talented she was. Also that she really only had one talent, and this was it. Fixing things.

"I'm not that lazy." Dim defended herself.

Glimmer just stared at her.

"Mallory is up river. How would we fight the current without getting caught?"

Again, the brass girl just stared at her.

"Alright, let's at least flip it over and see what we're working with."

And so they struggled to flip the small boat over to reveal a hole in the bottom. Dim went through her bag and found a small piece of metal that mostly covered it, and screwed it on. They flipped it back as they heard a commotion from the bank. Five of the brute's men appeared on the steep incline and across the water. They seemed to be arguing about who had to go down and kill them.

One tried throwing rocks, which came close, but did not quite reach them.

Dim decided that they might have a little more time, so she went back into her bag and pulled out various gears and a complicated rod looking thing.

Glimmer beeped a "what are you doing? Let's go."

Dim just muttered, "Get the oars," to her, and pointed towards them.

She touched the stag that Bromm had made and whispered, "help me if you can."

As if on queue, one henchman slipped and fell down the banking of the river. It was a rough fall and an even rougher landing. Dim's ankle twinged as she watched him. She hesitated a moment, but realized the man was not coming after them.

"Nice move!" One of his fellow henchmen yelled. The others followed suit until they noticed he wasn't moving at all.

Dim stopped paying attention at that point and attached the long rod to two shorter ones. She tried bending them or moving them inwards, to no avail. "It'll have to work." She said under her breath.

Glimmer beeped a 'what are you doing?'

"It's like your joints."

Some not understanding beeps came. Along with a dissatisfied whir. Being compared to a makeshift boat thingy was not sitting well with Glimmer.

"Your shoulders and elbows and stuff." the brass girl looked at her limbs. They did not look like a couple of rods connecting oars to a boat.

"Well," Dim started, "Not exactly. Just the same concept." She attached the oars and turned the front gear. The oars rowed.

Dim smiled. She may, well probably will, still die. But at least she's still trying not to.

The boat was moving and actually picking up speed as she got into a rhythm, turning the crank. They were outrunning the henchman who was following them. The other was trying to get down to the one who fell.

Glimmer was holding her hands to her ears and fanning them out as if to imitate antlers. It seemed appropriate, since Bromm would do that to taunt enemies occasionally.

He would stick his tongue out and give them a strawberry though, which, of course, Glimmer was incapable of. It was quite a sight watching the giant do that to a mob of remkins. They would get so mad for no reason and charge aimlessly. She missed Bromm terribly. He would have never let her go off on her own, well with Glimmer, like this.

She just hoped that they could reach the dam before anyone reached them on the left. She guessed port, since they were on a boat, side. If they could reach it, they had a fighting chance to reach Mallory's compound.

'But then what?' the gnome thought. 'What exactly could Mallory do? Even if she was on our side.'

She shook her head. She had to focus, at least for now. Bromm, even if he survived, the fire giants, which was incredibly improbable, was not here.

And he wasn't coming.

The others were not coming.

It was just the two of them and they knew their mission. Get to the lady who may or may not be their ally and figure it out from there.

Not the best plan at all.

But she had succeeded in worse before.

A few more men joined the taunted ones on what was now the bank on her right. No one seemed to be on the left side, which made her suspicious that it may all be a trap. That was the side closest to town and the side they had slid down.

Surely, the brute would have made it by now. Unless he was pulled to something more important. Did they catch the boys or the girls? Or both?

If they just had some way of communicating long distances, she could know where they were or if they had figured anything out. Even if it was just a quick message of some sort. Like 'done' or 'danger ahead' or the always needed 'it's a trap.' It could even just be a little picture or some little face, just to get the message across.

"Garrick would probably just use it to pick up girls." She laughed out loud. Glimmer gave her a strange look mid-taunt and Dim laughed again.

She would have to think on that one later. Right now they were getting close to the dam, the staircase and, most likely, the trap.

The gnome stopped turning the crank and turned to Glimmer. "You need to find a way out of here."

The brass girl was defiant. Beeping how she wasn't a chicken, and that she would not run and hide. She would go down in a fight if she had to go down. She put her fists up to demonstrate her point.

Dim missed most of it, but she got the gist. She crouched down to her level and looked her in the eyes. It threw her off a bit to have to do that.

"I know that you can fight, but I think this is a trap. If it is, we are going to be outnumbered. Badly."

Glimmer's fists went down dejectedly. She really wanted to punch someone.

"Even if it isn't a trap, we need to find out where everyone is. If you can sneak back and get Molly and Little Al, the three of you can scour the village and let people know what's going on."

She made a face.

"Yes, get them both. You may need to split up."

She made another face.

"He's not totally useless. Give him the easiest task."

She tilted her head.

Dim mimicked her look.

Glimmer gave another look that basically said, 'I don't think it's going to work. But okay.'

"Me neither. It's the best we got with no information." She looked around for a Glimmer sized escape hole. "There." She said, pointing to a small drainage pipe.

'Really?' her look said.

Dim raised her shoulders, "You may be able to get that cat-like-thing to pull you all."

Glimmer laughed at that. Then Dim joined in, picturing the three of them riding in on a chariot pulled by an eight-legged cat-like creature. Molly would have the reigns as Glimmer held a dagger as a sword in the air. Little Al would probably be trying to blow a horn.

"Do your best."

Glimmer saluted.

"Be careful."

She did Bromm's stag-antler salute to her and fell backwards into the water.

Chapter 23

Shiny Objects

She could see that the now five henchmen that were following her had stopped and were talking among themselves. She couldn't quite hear them enough to figure out what they were saying, but she was pretty sure it was about her.

Or lunch.

Probably her, but she decided that she was hungry and that they could just wait. She rummaged around in her pack to see if there was anything not too dirty that she could eat. She found some jerky that was wrapped pretty securely and pulled it out, watching as Glimmer made it to the pipe and giving her a thumbs up before crawling in.

"What are you doing there?" One of the henchmen finally asked.

"Eating." She yelled back between swallows. It wasn't a steak sandwich at the tavern, but since she couldn't remember when she last ate, it was pretty good.

"Are you coming soon?" The man yelled down.

"I am not really in a rush, no." She reached back into her bag and pulled out a canteen. It was full! Dim raised her hands in triumph. As she ate, she looked at the scenery. 'I really should come out here more.' She thought. It was nice, near the dam at least.

The henchmen paced back and forth. One tested the edge of the bank a couple of times, but after what happened to their friend, he seemed quite hesitant. She watched as they gathered into a huddle again and conferred. They seemed to be in disagreement over something.

"Say you?" another one yelled.

"Yes."

"Were you planning on coming up this side or the other?"

Dim finished the last of her jerky and took a sip from the canteen, placing everything back into her pack. It was an unassuming pack for the most part. As she dropped the canteen in, she realized that she had never seen it before today. She wondered who put it in.

"I was thinking the side you're not on, truthfully. Why do you ask?"

"Well, the dam looks wobbly. And of course, you saw what happened to Rolf." He said. "We're not sure we really want to risk crossing."

Dim turned the crank again and started for the steps on the opposite side of the dam. "Sorry. I think I'll try my luck on this side."

"No worries." He said, and a couple of them tested the dam.

She was almost at the steps when she saw one of the men about half way. He had to pass a really tricky part there, though, so she figured she'd beat him. She got close and grabbed her pack, climbing to the steps. "Careful up there." She yelled to the man.

"Thanks." He said, then nearly slipped.

"Close one."

"Yeah."

"Why don't you have archers?"

"Why would we need them?"

"Probably would have killed me by now."

The man stopped. "Yeah, maybe. I'll have to ask."

"Okay, bye now." and Dim waved. Hopefully, the men had forgotten all about Glimmer and they wouldn't bother her.

The man waved and then one of the others yelled at him and he began moving towards her again.

She climbed the steps and exited into the street.

Dashing into the nearest alley, Dim still felt that she was in a trap. There were many things she doubted herself on, many things she knew that she was naïve about, but knowing about being set up in a trap was not one of them.

It did not feel like her village anymore. She couldn't explain it, but it didn't. She saw the faces of the people walking as she stayed in the shadows that she recognized. Dim decided not to reach out to them.

They looked familiar and not. All at the same time.

There was something off about them. Not just some of them, all of them. Mr. Davies walked by, normally a timid man, seemingly afraid of anything that moved, but even he walked with that same dull look upon his face.

Not exactly zombies. Dim had met with them before. Or maybe a different kind. Regardless, she slunk back into the shadows and made herself as scarce as possible.

Her mission was to get to Mallory and take it from there. Trap or not.

So she trusted her instincts and stayed out of sight. Hopefully, the others were doing at least a little better than she was at this moment. She tried to hide from everyone, but it was like everyone who lived in the village was out tonight.

And all of them had the same blank, dead stare. Dim shivered when she saw them.

She tried to mimic the shadows, only using slight movements. As Garrick had taught her.

She also tried to remember that trick spell Earch had taught her once, when they were little. "It is a wonderful distraction," he had said, "If you are ever in need."

Drawing her daggers, with a bit of hesitation, she turned them in her hands. These were people she had known all her life. Not necessarily friends, but she did not want to have to kill them. If she had to, she would, but she hoped that it did not come to that.

Garrick's teachings seemed to do the trick as she made it the five blocks to where Mallory had her compound. Of course, now came the wall.

Bromm's training would help her here. A twenty-foot wall straight up looked quite formidable to the diminished gnome, but he had showed her to look for the divots and find the spots that she could find purchase. She surveyed the wall and found a spot, hidden away, that she could climb.

On top of the wall, she looked over at her surroundings. More henchmen wandered back and forth. It looked as if Mallory was not on their side after all, but the mission was the mission. Time to find out. She reached into her pack and found what she was looking for. A hook and rope to latch and climb back down the other side. She wished that the sun would move at some point. It still seemed to be before noon. Darkness would have helped a little.

She repelled down to the inside of the compound and flicked her wrist as Zaela had shown her one day. The hook came straight into her hand. Her ankle decided to play with her then, aching horribly. Dim tried to shake it off.

It all seemed easy. "Too easy." She laughed a little at that cliche, but it was true. She thought of what her mother once said, "It's like I'm the fly and all y'all's the honey."

She sat for a moment to clear her head. All this reminiscing was doing her no good.

And it reminded her of how alone she was right now. Normally, she did not mind being by herself. Enjoyed it mightily, usually. It was when she got her best thinking done.

But here, surrounded by enemies, walking into an obvious trap, and with everyone she knew dead, some sort of zombie, possibly in unknown peril or, in the case of Mrs. Appleby, maybe a traitor, she felt that she had no one.

She watched as the henchmen wandered through the yard, trying to get a read on any pattern they had. It seemed as if there wasn't one. But it developed eventually.

One guy was just doing laps. He'd come into view and then disappear for a good ten minutes and come back to where he began. Two were just standing there, sometimes talking, but usually not. Dim thought that one fell asleep at one point.

The last one on this side of the yard was the one that she had to worry about.

He seemed young, and in her view, was out to make a good impression. He was quite attentive, maybe overly so. Every movement or sound he went to investigate. Mainly birds or squirrels or other creatures. Once a leaf that was blowing in the wind. She would need to distract him to get anywhere near the house.

A light came on and she saw what appeared to be Mallory's shadow being thrown into a room. It was on the third floor and a bit to Dim's left.

A plan formed, but the timing had to be right. If the two talking henchmen were distracted enough and the attentive henchman could be preoccupied elsewhere, then she just needed to wait until the other guard was far enough away.

Dim figured that she only needed half a minute, give or take, to run the yard and climb to the balcony where the light had gone on. If her ankle held out, of course.

And if she could climb it.

It was not the best of plans, but also not the worst of plans. She waited for the lap-henchman had gone past and a few minutes longer. The two talking henchmen seemed quite useless. As long as she was quiet, she should be able to run across the yard before they noticed.

To distract the attentive one, she cast Earch's trick. She moved her fingers in the way he taught and whispered the chant.

At first, nothing happened, and she went to start again.

But then, a light. A light and a small murmur danced on the far wall. Dim whisked her fingers to and fro and watched as the light followed.

It was faint, but certainly visible, and she was having a bit of fun playing with it, until she saw the attentive one running towards it out of the corner of her eye. "Oh Hells." She mumbled, thinking that she nearly missed her mark.

Hearing the light of echo what she said from the light surprised her.

"I didn't know it did that, too." She said and heard it again through the light. She danced it around the building and the attentive one followed.

She was even more surprised to hear the attentive one yelling "who goes there?" but not from a distance, like she was right next to him.

Dim ran to the house as silently as the elf had taught her. The plan was coming together as the two other henchmen ignored her and were instead making fun of the attentive henchman as she climbed to the window where she had seen the old woman.

After reaching the balcony she tried to peer into the window, but it was not the cleanliest in all the village, and that was saying something. She could see movement from inside, and it seemed like it was only one person, so she knocked quietly on the glass.

The figure made its way over to the door. Dim pulled a dagger just in case the figure was either not Mallory or Mallory tried something.

It cracked, and the figure said, "Oh it's you," in a more than disappointed way.

"Glad to see you, too." Dim replied.

The woman let her in and closed the window quickly. "Sorry, I thought you'd be Esus."

"She sent me."

"By way of the sewer." The old woman said and waved her hand across her nose.

"Actually..." Dim started, but the sound of the brute's voice and three sets of footsteps interrupted her.

"What's gong on in there?" He yelled.

Dim hid as best she could in the curtains as Mallory went to the door. "Nothing, you big oaf."

He pushed past her. "You were talking to someone." He said.

"Just myself."

"I have been working for you for over a decade and never heard you talk to yourself."

"Worked. I fired you, remember?"

"How'd that work out for you?" He snickered. Dim heard the woman get pushed to the bed and footsteps come closer. "What's this then?"

The gnome squeezed her dagger in one hand, and the stag Bromm had given her in the other. 'I could use your help now, friend.' She thought to herself as she readied to either be stabbed or revealed.

One of the other henchman came close and flung the curtain aside. Dim thought about stabbing him, but did not have time.

She felt something push against her hand holding Bromm's stag. What came out was a spectral, full-sized stag that trampled first the henchman who had pulled the curtain and then the next. Its path through the room showed that something was there, but after it rammed the brute, it just disappeared.

The brute slammed first into the wall and then folded to the floor, bloodied and unmoving.

After the shock of what had happened wore off, Dim helped the old woman up. "You shouldn't have come here." Mallory said, grabbing her shoulder and pulling her close. "You're the one she needs."

The brute moaned. He wasn't attacking or running or even moving yet in the condition that he was in, but he was alive. That fact surprised Dim. He slammed into the wall pretty hard. There was a brute sized dent in it now.

The same couldn't be said for the other henchmen.

"Who?"

"Appleby."

"Dammit."

"I could have sworn you and Esus were up to something."

"Well, we were, but she all 'fell in love' and had a 'change of heart.' Pathetic and somehow endearing at the same time." Mallory said, rushing Dim to the door. "That dope and Appleby beat us to it, though."

"What is going on with everyone and why do they need me?" Dim dug in her heels, literally.

Mallory kept trying to push the gnome, but she wasn't moving. At least by the old woman's strong, but diminished by age, shove.

"My friend died because of this, and that's on me. I need to fix this." She looked at the woman. "I need to at least try." She looked at the old woman with a tinge of pity and a heaping load of beg. She needed help.

"I don't really know much." Mallory said, sitting on her bed. "Appleby has the box and can't make it work like you."

"But why are all the people..."

"Zombies. I do not know." She rubbed her temples. "After you left. After the fire. I guess when Appleby got the box, anyone who did not side with her became like that."

"You're not."

"Again, I don't know exactly what's going on."

"What do we know?"

Mallory looked down. "We have to get out of here. Before someone comes. Or he gets up."

"I am not going anywhere with you until I know what you know."

"That'll be quick." She said, "I left the village when you left. I had some business to take care of. When I came back, everyone was..."

"Zombies."

"Zombies." She nodded. "Except most of my work-ers."

"Henchmen."

"So you say. They lured me in and basically im-prisoned me in my own home. Then you came in the window and did something that blasted them." She thumbed over to the brute and his underlings. "All they said is 'we need the gnome.' I'm guessing that is you."

"Maybe." Dim said.

"I haven't seen another gnome in ages."

"I have." Dim was a bit more worried that it was the other gnome that was needed, and not her. What the old woman had said checked out with what Dim had experienced. She let her lead the way out.

Chapter 24

A Mild Breakdown

Now Dim had no genuine hope of ever getting out of that house without being killed or captured, but she went along with Mallory just the same. So far, it seemed that as long as she kept trying, something would get her out of a jam.

"How'd you do that?" Mallory asked as she stepped over the brute and into the hall, looking down both directions of the hallway.

"I don't know." She answered, fingering the stag carving around her neck. "It just happened."

"Hopefully, you can make it happen again if need be." Around them, it sounded like twenty men were coming. Mallory seemed, at that moment, to be studying her wall. "Here." She pointed at a quite nondescript part.

Dim followed the woman into the hallway. She was pushing on various parts of the wall.

"What are you doing?" Dim asked. The men were getting closer and the woman just kept muttering about it being here somewhere. The gnome pulled her other dagger from its scabbard and readied herself.

With a final push, Mallory found the correct brick, and it slid into the rest of the wall, revealing a door. "Help me."

"Ooh, secret passage." Dim said as the two women pushed the wall open and filed in to the tight fit, struggling to close the wall again.

"There!" they heard one man yell as the door locked into place. Mallory then pulled a lever, and they heard a click from where they just came through. The men were banging on the wall.

Mallory caught her breath. "Shouldn't we be going?" Dim asked.

"Just a moment, dear. I am not as young as I once was." She leaned against the wall, catching her breath and holding her chest. "They can't get through without tearing down the wall. It's locked."

"Are you okay?"

The woman laughed, "I will be. Haven't had this much excitement in a long time."

"So, where does my newest tunnel lead?" Dim asked, "Please don't say the sewer."

The old woman gave her a look to confirm this. "Oh Hells, no!" Dim said. Mallory laughed.

"No, no," she said, but kept laughing. "That look on your face was almost worth all this hassle."

"Hilarious." the gnome said, but actually laughed as well.

"Once you get a bit of money and power, you don't go into the sewer anymore." She looked at the gnome. "You seem to forget that I grew up here."

"You weren't here much. At least since I've been here."

Mallory pushed herself from the wall. "Yes, true." She said and started walking. "I remember when your mother took you in, though."

"Really?"

"Yeah, we were quite close, your mom, me, and Appleby. When we were young." She looked like she was in the past at that moment.

"You didn't come to the funeral." Dim said.

"I was there. I just didn't want to cause a spectacle. Stayed in the back." Mallory said, "I came back later, after everyone left. Except you."

"I stayed quite a long time."

The old woman laughed. "That you did."

"What happened to you three?" the gnome asked as they rounded a corner and finally came to a door.

"I don't know. Life, years, business, men." She looked at the gnome, "or at least one man."

"My dad?" Dim's face showed

"Don't look so shocked. Talented, kind, good-looking." She watched as Dim's head tilted to the side, slowly.

Dim made a gagging noise. "So you let a man break you up."

"Not really." She looked to be in the past again. "Your mom was happy. Me and Appleby kind of drifted apart, without your mother holding us together. She was kind of our 'friend glue', so to speak. We'd catch up now and then. It seems to just be how life works sometimes. I guess it's hard for a daughter to see that in her dad. Plus, he was much older by the time you showed up."

They opened the door and looked out.

Waves upon waves of people were walking by Mallory's 'secret' exit, all with the same blank look on their faces.

This was no longer just their village.

"What the Hells?" Dim whispered. It was all that she could get out.

"Seems Appleby has been busy." Mallory went back inside and scrounged around for something. She came back with a sword belt that appeared to tip her to one side. "Guess we're in for a fight now."

Dim covered her mouth, looking at the woman to stifle her laugh. It didn't work. "You can stay here if you want, doesn't look like I'm getting too far, anyway."

"Not a chance. I've been keeping out of the dirty work for too long. If someone needs to take down Appleby, I might as well be there." She limped with the weight of her sword. She winked at the gnome, "Or, at least try."

"Suit yourself." Dim said and walked out. The woman grabbed her arm.

"I should have let you be. For that, I am sorry. I was jealous of your quick success and sadly, territorial. But truthfully, I should have just let you take over here." She looked the gnome in the eyes. "If not for the village, for you mother. She was an exceptional woman, and a better friend."

"And the best mom." Dim added. "Thank you, but that's all in the past. We got some work to do."

"And you need a bath." Mallory said, hand on her sword.

"And I need a bath." Dim said and pulled her daggers, yet again. She wondered if they were tiring of being unsheathed and yet not tasting blood. "And a large bit of wine."

The two women, and elder business woman, recently imprisoned in her own home and a tiny gnome, who reeked of the foulest of odors, limped together towards the pack of zombie-like villagers, waiting, and ready, to be attacked. They touched each other's hand for just a moment. Neither one would have been able to tell you who had reached out first, but they had touched briefly, looked each other in the eye and nodded. Then they ran out to fight what they thought was their final battle.

No one, not a single villager, acknowledged their presence.

The two had run towards the massive line of people, basically ready to die. About half way there, they both stopped. Mallory more because she was out of breath, not having properly judged the distance, Dim more out of confusion.

The gnome stopped and tilted her head.

"Why do you do that?" Mallory asked between catching her breath.

Her head tilted the other way towards her. "Do what?"

"Never mind." She said.

"You okay?" The gnome said. She put her hand on her shoulder and waited. Mallory tried to talk a few more times and then just put up one finger, telling her to wait.

They were in a small field with hundreds of people from this and nearby villages just walking in a line, five or six deep, towards Appleby's farm. Dim had been sure that they would attack them, not that she wanted to fight. She was too tired, her ankle killed, and as far as she knew, these were innocent villagers.

She had just, well, expected that they would when they saw a gnome with two daggers and an old woman with a sword running towards them. But nope.

Mallory seemed to catch her breath. "I will be. Why are they not attacking us?"

"No clue."

"They're walking towards Appleby's."

Dim looked at the group. "Looks like it. Have you noticed that the sun hasn't moved in a while?"

Mallory looked towards the sun. "Ah, now that you mention it. Strange." She looked back at Dim after a moment. "Should we join them?" She shrugged her shoulders and seemed ready to go. Her breathing had slowed, and the red had, at least, lightened in her face. Dim looked at her and found it hard to imagine that she had feared this woman about an hour ago.

The gnome thought for a second, rubbed her chin and just said, "Might as well."

And so they did. The two sheathed their weapons and pushed their way into the middle of the pack, trying to keep themselves out of view from the henchmen as best they could.

Dim and Mallory elbowed each other and giggled as they marched along with the others. It's all they could do to hold themselves together. The ridiculousness of what they were doing, walking into Appleby's den with her newfound zombie army, was too much for them to fathom.

They straightened themselves out as they saw some of Mallory's former henchmen came by.

Dim saw one henchman trying to get her attention as they tried to blend in. She pushed Mallory closer to the other side, but he was waving at her in an attempted, but not very effective, inconspicuous way. She nodded to him, but he did not look familiar.

"Hey." He said and pushed in between the zombies next to them.

"Hi."

"Remember me?"

"Not really." He looked a tad bit sad at this. "It really has been a long day." She added to maybe make him feel a little better.

"Who's this?" Mallory asked her. Dim shrugged.

The henchman pretended to be straddling something and then put his hands up like he was falling while they marched to the gnome's doom, or whatever was happening.

"Ah, you made it across. Good for you." Dim turned to Mallory, "He's one of yours, I think. He was trying to catch me on the river."

"Didn't do a great job." She said, "Did I hire you?"

"You're Madame Mallory! No, we never met." He reached out to shake her hand, noticed that she had no intention of being touched, and pulled away quickly. "Esus hired me a few months back. I thought you were captured, or dead."

"One of those. Does everybody think that?" Mallory asked him.

"Not everyone." He lowered his head. "But it doesn't really matter. None of us had much of a choice in the end."

"What do you mean?" the gnome asked.

"Well," He looked at them, his eyes sunken and distant, "they ordered us to round up the villagers."

"And you went along with it?" Dim said, a bit too loud. Mallory put her arm on her shoulder to say, 'let him finish.'

The henchman lowered his head again, "Not all of us, at least not at first. Some of us wanted to get the order from you, or at least Esus, not..."

"Mormoth."

"Yeah," he continued, "some of us went to ask to see you, but..." he paused.

"It's okay."

"No, no, it isn't. They killed two of us on the spot. 'For disobeying orders.'" He made air quotes to emphasize the point. "Another, who tried to run, they made her into one of them." He thumbed towards the zombies. "After that, well, we all just fell in line, hoping for an opportunity to escape."

"What's your name, son?" Mallory asked. Her tone took Dim aback. The woman she thought of as being Mean Madame Mallory could be quite soft when needed.

"Rex."

"Well, Rex, maybe you can help us end this." The mob turned onto Appleby's road. "We need to get in there without getting noticed."

"I may be able to help with that."

The plan was actually quite simple. Rex, the henchman, was a sentry for the entire operation and in a prime spot to help. You see, Mrs. Appleby had a barn that was close to the road leading in, and there was, which was unusual for the time and the place, an entryway from the barn to the house.

All they had to do was get close to the barn, make a run about ten meters without being seen, and bam, they were in. Rex would create a distraction and no problem. They are in the barn.

What exactly was in the barn and what they might face there was a completely different story.

"Did you ask about the archers?" She said. Dim really wanted to ask about Glimmer and if they had gone after her, but also did not want to remind them of her if she got away. She did not totally trust Rex.

"Oh yeah. I guess we have some."

"Oh, nice."

"Apparently we weren't supposed to kill you." He shrugged his shoulders. "They probably should have told us that part, huh?"

"Probably." Dim laughed.

"I should go. That's my spot." He nodded his head to a clearing near the barn. "Wait about thirty seconds or so after I get there. I'll think of something."

"Okay, take care."

"You too, I mean um..." His face told her that he just now was realizing how weird this was, so he added, "I really hope that you survive."

"Me too." Dim said.

"Me three." Mallory said and Rex was off.

"I wouldn't do that." Mallory said.

"Do what?" She did not notice that she was ripping at one of her fingernails with her teeth.

"Chew your nails."

"I am not..." she started, then realized she was.

"You've been through a sewer."

"And the cobolds."

"And the cobolds, wait you did not tell me about those."

"Didn't really have the time."

Mallory swatted at Dim's hands. "There is no way those should be in your mouth."

"Can't help it." Dim wanted to go on. She wanted to explain how sick of following everyone else's plans she was. From Gallila to Zaela to Mallory to now some random dude named Rex, she was quite done with all of it. Especially just following along as others called the shots. "I am pissed."

"Why?"

"Nothing I have done in the past, like year, or whatever, has been my decision. Except to sit around and not do anything besides build stuff. Everything else I have been dragged into and it's gone to, well, the sewer."

"So, stop." Mallory said. "Walk away and go home."

"I can't do that."

"Why not? It's your choice."

"My friends..."

"Oh, they'll either survive or not. They may be dead already. We don't know." Mallory took a breath. She knew she overstepped a bit there. "The truth is, people get along or not on their own accord. If they survive, they survive, if they die, they die. You are probably not going to be the difference. Unless you choose to be. There is no chosen one who saves everyone."

Dim stopped walking and looked at the woman.

"You are not that special. Neither am I. We just need to choose a path and do our best." She looked to where Rex had gone and saw a light. "That's our cue. You coming?"

Dim waited a moment and let the old woman's words sink in. She could just walk away and things may play out however they did, and she may be of no consequence to what transpired. Or maybe she could.

Either way, she had to see what had happened to her friends. At least, maybe, she could help them.

Chapter 25

The Dollhouse and a Bit of Cheese

Rex's fire did not last long, but it accomplished its goal. It actually worked better than they had thought, as not only did it grab the attention of the henchmen but also the zombies, who turned towards it.

Unintended or not, the zombie mob turned closer to the barn, giving Dim and Mallory a shorter sprint to it. This was good, as Dim was exhausted physically and emotionally by this point and Mallory was just out of shape for this sort of thing. They made it without incident.

Once inside, well, that was a different story altogether.

The two women waited as one of them (Mallory) caught her breath for about a minute and then they made their way to the door. They did not sneak or try to cover their path.

This, in hindsight, was a mistake. As they reached the door, in darkness and quite nonchalant like, they saw four figures waiting for them.

Garrick, Earch, Zaela and Esus.

Now Mallory had met them all before, although, except for Esus, it was quite a brief encounter. She knew right away, however, that something was wrong. Dim did not realize this quite as quick, waving to her friends and saying a quick "hi." She realized right after that, though, when her so-called 'boyfriend' decided to shoot a magic dart-like thing into her chest.

"What the...." she got out, although the "Hells" part never escaped her mouth. The missiles took her breath from her and she fell hard.

As she hit the floor, she realized what Rex had said was true. They did not want her dead. If they had wanted her dead, a zombified Earch could have struck her much harder. Or Garrick, Zaela or Esus could have snuck up and stabbed her easily.

No, they needed her. But why?

She looked at Mallory and saw that the woman had drawn her sword and was about to be struck down by Esus. "Stop!" She yelled and held one of her daggers to her own throat. Esus and the others paused.

"Kill her and I will do it!" the gnome said, getting a bit over zealous and nicking herself to bleed a little.

Her zombie friends stopped immediately and turned to her.

"What are you doing?" Mallory said.

"They need me." Dim said back. "Alive."

"Why?"

Dim shrugged. "Maybe the box?"

Mallory sheathed her sword and raised her hands. Dim kept her dagger close to her throat. "Take us to Appleby." She said. And they obeyed.

Appleby and a battered Mormoth were sitting in her dining room, waiting eagerly for Dim's arrival. On seeing Mallory, the brute lunged, but Appleby stopped him. "No need, no need." She said to him. "She is.... irrelevant."

Dim looked at Mallory and tried to convey that she should not react. It must be tough for a woman of her power and influence to not react to being called irrelevant, but at this point in time, it was crucial that she did not. The gnome wasn't sure that all of that got across to Mallory, but the woman gritted her teeth and said nothing. "Why do you need me?" Dim said to her former friend, who not so long ago had welcomed her as family, but now seemed dead set to torment her through her real friends.

Appleby looked at Dim over her glasses. "Need? I don't need you at all." Her tone was irritable, but she took a deep breath and straightened her blouse. Her eyes were wild, staring into nothingness.

"What if I just wanted to invite my old friend, Nay, my family over?"

"Probably could have been easier ways to invite me than chasing me through a sewer, don't ya think?" Dim said, "I may even have bathed first. Now what do you NEED, so I can get my friends out of here?" With that, Earch and Garrick doubled over in pain, screaming through even their zombie state. Dim went to Earch, but the brute stepped between.

"There you go, upsetting and misunderstanding me. I don't NEED anyone." She again calmed herself, and the wailing from the boys subsided. "But you may put your friends out of their misery. If you cooperate."

The brute struck Garrick in the head with the hilt of his sword, and the rogue fell over like a sack. Again Dim tried to rush to him, but the brute pointed his sword at Earch's chest.

"One more step, missy. Just one more."

Dim stopped, her head lowered. "What do you want me to do?"

"I love when I get good help." Mrs. Appleby pulled the wooden box out of her pocket and held it up to Dim. "Show me how to make this work. Or open it. Or whatever you did."

"I don't know how it works." Dim said softly. Immediately, Zaela succumbed to pain. "I really don't. I was told that is a compass. That is all." Zaela stood at attention again.

"But you powered the tools."

"I never knew how that worked. I built them, Earch cast a spell, and the box seemed to just make it work."

"But, it told me to get you." Appleby's eyes glared at the gnome, "It told me to bring the Dim to it." The woman was pacing back and forth. "I did what you said." She said to the box, "Leave me alone now." Apparently, it was not leaving her alone as she yelled something incoherent into her living room, screamed and threw the box at the wall.

It both smashed into a thousand pieces and bounced uninjured off of the wall, somehow at the same time.

"What is happening?" Mallory asked, then looked at the brute.

Dim watched as the thousands of pieces of box slowly disappeared, or were never there, or were reassembling. She really couldn't tell once they were gone, and the box was whole again, or still. The wooden box seemed to hum and glow for her. She walked towards it.

"Hold on a minute, miss." The brute said. Dim seemed to stop and keep going and walk faster all at the same time. "I said stop!" He yelled and held his sword to Mallory.

The three Dims melted back into one and stopped. "I did." She said, but it echoed from the three mouths until they were one.

"Did you do this?" Mallory yelled at the Mormoth.

"Do what? I do not know what's going on. I was just paid to steal the box by that woman from that woman." he pointed towards Appleby and then Dim. "Then it seemed to let me control people."

"The zombies?" Mallory asked.

"Yes."

"Why?"

"Seems to give people what they want, fuel their desires." Dim said.

"Why?" asked the brute.

"To get what it wants."

"Why's she a blubbering idiot, then?" Mallory asked.

"Look closer." Dim pointed to Mrs. Appleby.

All three of them stood still and stared at the woman. What had been one, blubbering, idiotic Mrs. Appleby, slowly became multiple, blubbering, idiotic Mrs. Applebys. All of them yelling and having a conversation with someone or something in the living room.

"I did what you asked." One Mrs. Appleby, that Dim tried hard not to lose focus on. "Leave me alone."

She seemed to listen to whatever was talking. "No, no. I can not do that."

Another pause. "Please, no."

"What the Hells is this?" Mallory asked Dim.

"Inter dimensional cheese melting." Dim said.

"What?" the brute and Mallory said at the same time while Appleby was still blubbering into the other room. She seemed to have some sort of conversation.

"The box is a compass or map to the hut. The hut can travel to different worlds." She tried to explain. "In between is the melted cheese."

They both looked at her as if she was crazy.

"Sorry, that's how it was explained to me. It made more sense when he said it."

"Who?" asked the brute.

Before she could answer, Mrs. Appleby said "fine." to whatever it was that she was talking to and walked towards the box and picked it up.

Dim tackled the woman as Mallory pulled her sword and blocked the brute's first swing at her. The box levitated for a moment out of Appleby's hand and seemed to float in the air for what, to Dim, felt like an eternity. It was, of course, not an eternity, but just a split second or two. It then fell and did not fall at the same time, deciding, Dim guessed, on which reality it wanted to choose. Eventually it settled on floating in midair and pointing into the room where Mrs. Appleby had been talking to whatever she had been talking to.

Now, battles like this can be deceiving because it is all relative to how you perceive the battle itself. Madame Mallory, for instance, may tell the tale of how she combated the brute for a few minutes. To her, this would be accurate, as she was in the battle. To the brute, or an outside observer, however, it lasted about eight seconds.

And it really should not have lasted that long.

Mallory blocked the brute's first swing, which astounded him. It wouldn't have, if he had known that she was once actually a very renowned swords woman. That was a long time ago, however, and she was quite out of practice.

He also outweighed her by quite a bit.

The woman fell back from the force and found herself against a wall. She even partially blocked the second swing, which cut her and slammed her against said wall and dropped her to the floor.

The brute then stabbed the prone woman below her shoulder blade. Luckily for her, this did not kill her. Unluckily, it caused her quite a bit of pain going forward in her life.

The resulting eight second delay counteracted what Mallory had told Dim earlier because without that eight seconds, the brute probably would have just stabbed Dim, maybe sliced her a few more times and everyone, except of course Dim and probably her zombified friends, would have gone on their merry little way.

Because of those eight seconds, however, the box decided it did not want to work for Mrs. Appleby anymore, and the two women were basically wrestling to get to the floating box first.

Although they were, at least at first, quite useless. Garrick, Earch, Zaela and Esus began to think on their own. There were a lot of 'what's going on?' and 'Where are we?' at the start. A bit of a daze, to be sure and not really anything that would help Dim and Mallory fight Appleby and the brute to be sure.

But explosions rained down upon all the people outside. At first, the gnome had no clue what was going on, but then she figured it out.

It was her grenades that she had removed from her bag after the duke incident.

The tinkers were coming.

Many things happened at that moment. Dim could hear the battle outside, along with the explosions of her grenades. She was not sure if the tinkers were being effective at all, but they certainly were causing quite a commotion.

The brute seemed torn as to what to do. Out of the corner of her eye, she saw him simultaneously run out the door and leave them, kill her friends, kill Mallory and run towards her and Mrs. Appleby. She had no idea which of these things was actually happening. Maybe they all were, depending on the universe she was looking at.

In the end, all his forms blended together and she saw him running towards the door.

As he opened it, however, the two women touched the box, and it began to vibrate and glow. The light grew and grew and flowed out the windows and through the door the brute had opened.

He turned around and immediately began to walk back into the living room.

At the same time, the sounds of fighting outside slowly faded. Except for the explosions. The first of the zombified villagers walked through the door and followed the brute.

Soon, a long line of zombies and henchmen were moving past the fighting women to get into the living room.

Dim looked towards their path, and succumbed, at least for the moment, into insanity.

What she saw was quite hard to explain. Everyone was walking towards the dollhouse on her living room table. They were both shrinking to fit into its tiny door and not shrinking to fit at the same time. The people also were transforming from one person to another in front of her eyes.

One, she saw, was at first Mr. Nieves, then a child she never had seen before, then a henchman, then the tavern owner.

Then he shrunk, but did not shrink, down to the size of the door and walked in. Many others followed him, doing the same thing.

Dim's grip on the box loosened, and Appleby pulled it away.

She began feeling the need to walk into the dollhouse. It was the only thought that was in her head. The only thing that seemed possible at that moment.

Dim walked towards the living room, joining the line of people as they continued to morph from one person to another and blindly walked towards the dollhouse, as one after the other entered it.

The realization struck Mrs. Appleby as she secured the box and finally looked at what was happening. Everyone that she had ever known was walking towards and into the dollhouse.

"No." She mouthed.

"No!" she yelled. "This is not what I wanted. This is not what you promised me!"

A grenade smashed through a window and exploded against the wall, crumbling the doorway to the living room. The zombies who were not injured by the blast, along with Dim, began to clear it to make their way through.

A small, metal head peeked through the window, making a face that could only be described as 'oopsy.'

Glimmer then whirred and beeped to the other tinkers to get in there, and they did in style, much as Dim had envisioned it. The cat-like thing was pulling the wagon as Little Al held the reins. Molly was standing in the back with a grenade in each hand, ready to throw in any direction needed.

What the tinker saw, and the other tinkers saw, was not exactly what has been described to you, though. What Molly, Little Al and Glimmer saw was exactly what was happening in this world, with none of the 'melted cheese,' so to speak.

The brute was headed for the door, and almost stepped on the cat-like-thing to get there. Garrick was still laying out on the floor. The other friends and Esus were just throwing up in the corner. Random people were trying to clear the crumbled door and trampling each other to get into the living room. They could recognize some of them.

The farm lady, as they called Mrs. Appleby, was pushing Dim aside in the corner, clawing at her face and had recently soiled herself. Screaming something.

Glimmer looked at Molly and shrugged. Molly shrugged back, as did Little Al, even though no one had shrugged at him. Glimmer looked into the living room and saw the village people shrinking to doll size and entering the house through the front door.

The brute fell back into the room with Rex not far behind, having stabbed his former boss through.

"What the Hells!" He said and quickly became incoherent to all but the tinkers.

"Stop the dollhouse!" Dim said, as she simultaneously died a thousand deaths and lived a thousand lives in an instant. The tinkers only saw her plunge her dagger into Mrs. Appleby's breast.   ·

Little Al steered the cat-like thing through an opening in the doorway and straight towards the dollhouse. Molly pushed it as they passed.

The dollhouse, for a brief moment, began to glow and change. How it was changing, exactly, was indescribable. It seemed to flicker in and out of existence and change shape and structure, but also not change at all. As it changed, it was still the same and was always like that. Until it changed again and was also always like that.

It continued to not change as Dim grabbed the wooden box and held it. Moving closer to the doll-house.

She felt the vibration and the hum.

She felt its comfort again, but she knew now that it was a false feeling. It was something that may give temporary relief to the difficulties in your life, but if you let it, it would abuse your soul.

She intended not to let it this time.

Earch watched, mesmerized, while Zaela and Esus stood by. Finally, the dollhouse fell from its table as Molly intended. It both crashed onto the floor, breaking into a million pieces, and disappeared immediately when she touched it.

If you had seen it, you would have said that both happened.

In reality, or multiple realities, both did.

Chapter 26

A Well Earned Bath

Dim looked at her fallen former friend, a woman who had helped her parents in the past as they had helped her. Mrs. Appleby was a broken shell of her former self. She lay huddled in the corner, babbling, bleeding, and twitching. A wooden box twinkled in and out of existence in her hand.

Dim looked at the box in her own hand and saw it flickering in and out of existence, as well. She focused on her box as she saw Mrs. Appleby focusing.

She felt the woman's will come through, trying desperately to break her own.

The gnome pushed all thoughts out and concentrated on the box, willing it solid. The woman's thoughts buried into her own and, for a moment, the box in her hand disappeared.

"No!" the gnome yelled and envisioned it there, solid, vibrating as it had done before.

"No!" Mrs. Appleby screamed as her box flickered away and Dim's solidified. She had won. Or depending on your point of view, lost. She looked at the woman and saw her shaking in the fetal position, clutching at a box that wasn't there. Tears and sweat beaded, her face unrecognizable. Her eyes were wild-wide and staring.

"No! This is not... You promised.... What I... Me... Me... me... mmm..." The rest was hard to hear, or at least recognizable as speech.

Dim looked at the others. The zombie villagers were trying to figure out where they were, or at least, what had happened on the last day or so.

Rex and Esus were binding Mallory's shoulder as best they could, with her pushing them away at every opportunity. Telling them to "stop babying" her.

Zaela was tending to Garrick.

The tinkers were celebrating by throwing grenades out a window and watching people run away.

Earch was staring at the gnome.

"I think she's broken." Dim pointed at Mrs. Appleby.

Earch came to her and gave her a hug.

"Don't, I smell."

"Yes, you do." He said, but did not let go. Dim let him and hugged him back, slipping the box into her pocket.

"Are you okay?" Earch asked.

"No." Dim said. She was most certainly not okay. She felt as far from okay as she possibly could be. "But, I will be."

"What are we going to do about her?" Dim asked as she looked at the poor woman laying on the floor.

"I'll see that she gets the best care possible." Mallory said, pushing Rex away from her for the hundredth time.

"Why?" asked Garrick, coming a bit more to his senses.

"She is, or at least was, my friend. I owe it to her to try." she looked at Dim. "A friend once told me that we have to at least try."

"You're a better person than I." He said. "I need a drink."

"I hear ya on that." Zaela said.

"Get me to the tavern and I will pour all you want." The tavern owner said, which shocked Dim, as she was sure that he was one of the ones who had walked into the dollhouse.

"You coming?" They said to Dim.

Dim walked out into the sunshine and looked at the sky. The sun seemed to have moved again. She touched the box in her pocket and it hummed a soothing hum. "It's been a bad day. I'm going home for a bottle of wine and a warm bath."

And that's what she did.

Well, not exactly. She went to her parents' old house instead. She did this for two reasons.

The first was that she had, a long time ago, set up running, and heated, water at her parents' house one year as a present to them. It was the only house that she had ever known about to have actual running water. Many had wells and such, but she had built custom pipes and ran the lake water directly into the house.

She had thought about making this a business once, but she hated digging. Digging was extremely hard. No fun at all, so she nixed that idea.

The second reason was that maybe no one, not even the tinkers or Earch, would think that she would go there. This was one night that she did not want to talk to anyone. She loved them all, but this day was too much. So, even though she had to turn the water on and light a fire and deal with long suppressed memories before taking her coveted bath, she still went there.

With the water on and the fire going, with the pipes flushed and the bathroom (kind of) cleaned, she poured a glass of wine and placed the bottle nearby. She took a sip and let out a sigh.

She shed her robe and slowly lowered herself into the hot water.

Dim, the tinker gnome, took a long, hot bath and drank her wine.